"Now, what can I do for you, Sherm?"

"I'd like to speak to you for a moment." He glanced at the woman sipping cider. "Alone if you don't mind."

"Certainly. Please excuse me, Mrs. James, and thank you for the dance."

Sherman led the doctor through the milling crowd and out the side door into a deserted alley. After a few steps he turned to his friend. "Tom, I want to know what your intentions are concerning Miss Casey."

"Miss Casey? Th   I have no intentions regardir   uestion, Sherm?"

"I just—" The   his hair. "I heard—someo   ing the teacher. That it wa

"Well, someone was mistaken. I like Marian Casey. She's an asset to our community. But no, I am not courting her."

A flood of relief washed over Sherman, bringing a smile to his face. "Are you seeing her home tonight?"

"Joanna and I are supposed to." The doctor cocked his head to one side. "Are you interested in Miss Casey?"

Sherman cleared his throat. "I might be."

"Why don't you speak up? Ask her if you can come calling."

"I would if she'd give me a chance. Tom, she runs from me like I was contagious."

"Mariah Casey is reserved, but I haven't found her to be unfriendly. If we put our heads together maybe we can come up with a way for the two of you to get better acquainted."

M. J. CONNER is the pen name for sisters Mildred Colvin and the late Jean Norval. Mildred Colvin and her husband have three children, one son-in-law, one daughter-in-law, and two grandchildren. Mildred writes inspirational romance novels because in them the truth of God's presence, even in the midst of trouble, can be portrayed. Her desire is to continue the ministry started with her sister by writing stories that uplift and encourage.

Books by M. J. Conner

HEARTSONG PRESENTS
HP435—Circle of Vengeance
HP643—Escape to Sanctuary

Mariah's Hope

M. J. Conner

Heartsong Presents

To the editorial staff at Peterson Ink. Working with you all is a blessing.

A note from the Author:
I love to hear from my readers! You may correspond with me by writing:

M. J. Conner
Author Relations
PO Box 721
Uhrichsville, OH 44683

ISBN 1-59789-037-5

MARIAH'S HOPE

All scripture quotations are taken from the King James Version of the Bible.

All of the characters and events in this book are fictitious. Any resemblance to actual persons, living or dead, or to actual events is purely coincidental.

Our mission is to publish and distribute inspirational products offering exceptional value and biblical encouragement to the masses.

PRINTED IN THE U.S.A.

one

Willow Creek, Ohio, 1893

" 'Who can find a virtuous woman? for her price is far above rubies.' " The minister's face was solemn as he closed his worn, black Bible and faced the handful of mourners standing around the open grave.

"We are gathered today to celebrate the home going of Margaret Casey, devoted wife of Charles, loving mother of Mariah. I never knew my predecessor, Pastor Charles Casey, or Mrs. Casey personally," the black-garbed pastor continued, "but I have been told that before the tragic accident that took her husband's life and left her an invalid, she worked tirelessly at Brother Casey's side ministering to his flock."

Mariah Casey, standing apart from the other mourners, the March wind whipping her black skirt against her legs, listened as the minister continued to expound on the virtues of the woman lying in the closed casket. A woman who, by his own admission, he never knew.

After the final prayer, Mariah left the cemetery and walked the short distance to her home. Turning in at the front gate, she strolled around the yard inspecting her flowerbeds. The yellow daffodils were already lifting their cheerful faces to the sun, and soon the tulips would be in bloom. By midsummer the yard would be ablaze with color. Mariah pulled a few weeds, then walked up the front steps, crossed the porch, and unlocked the front door. Stepping across the threshold from the bright spring sunshine into the perpetual gloom of the dark parlor, she hesitated for a moment, waiting for the querulous, demanding voice that had greeted her return home every day for the past eighteen years since her father's death. The house was silent.

Two days ago she had come home from school to find her mother lying dead on the floor. Now Margaret Casey rested in the cemetery beside a man she despised—her hateful voice forever stilled—and Mariah was free.

She went to her bedroom and changed into old clothes. After carefully brushing the black suit she had worn to the funeral and hanging it in the wardrobe, she sat down on the edge of the bed.

With her mother gone, she was free to rip down the heavy drapes and let the sunshine in. She could rehang the mirrors her mother had demanded she pack away after the accident. There were so many things she could do, but sitting alone in the gloom of her own bedroom, she knew she would do nothing to the dark, oppressive house. Though she had spent all of her thirty-five years in this house, it had never been her home. It never would be. Twin tears splashed on her clasped hands, and she impatiently brushed them away. Crying never accomplished anything.

She slipped to her knees beside her bed. *Father, please look on me with favor and hear my prayer. I'm not asking for a husband and children. I know it's too late for that, but please send me a friend. Someone who doesn't care that I'm tall and skinny and unattractive. Someone who can see beyond my outward appearance and love me for what's in my heart.*

&

Cedar Bend, Kansas

Walking out of Harris's Mercantile, Sherman Butler almost collided with Gladys Jacobs, who was hurrying into the store.

"Mr. Butler, I have the answer to your problems," she said without preamble. "This morning I was talking to the Lord about how your Carrie was getting married and how we were going to need a new teacher here in Cedar Bend. The solution to our problem came to me just as clear as day." She looked up at Sherman, her blue eyes magnified by the gold-rimmed glasses perched on the end of her sharp nose. "My cousin Mariah would be perfect for the position. I have her address right here."

Gladys Jacobs was a fine woman, but she had a tendency to be a bit overbearing at times. Sherman inwardly groaned as she extracted a scrap of paper from her handbag. "Mariah has taught at the same school in Ohio for almost twenty years."

He took the paper she thrust at him and glanced at it before putting it in his shirt pocket. "We have already contacted several highly qualified people about the position."

"Not a one of those people has responded, is that not correct?"

"Not yet," Sherman agreed. "But I'm sure we'll get a favorable reply soon."

"Time is running out, Mr. Butler." She straightened her narrow shoulders. "I spoke to Doctor Brady this morning. He feels my cousin Mariah would be perfect for us."

A wry smile twisted Sherman Butler's mouth. Gladys Jacobs was single-minded and tenacious when her mind was set on a project, but he had to admit, she got things done. "Your cousin may not be interested in giving up her present position and relocating to Kansas."

"I haven't seen Mariah since she was a small child, but we have corresponded for several years. I fear she is a lonely, unhappy woman." A thoughtful expression crossed Gladys's sharp features. "My uncle was a minister—a wonderful man to be sure—but more involved with feeding his flock than nurturing his only child. Mariah was a young girl when we left Ohio almost thirty years ago. Even then, Margaret—as vain and selfish a woman as ever lived—made no secret of the fact that her daughter was a disappointment to her. Many years ago my aunt and uncle were involved in an accident. Uncle Charles was killed and Margaret was badly injured. Since then Mariah has taught school and cared for her mother. She wrote me several months ago to tell me Margaret had passed away. Mariah has no family in Willow Creek and, reading between the lines of her letters, not a single friend."

She paused to catch her breath, and Sherman began to ease around her. "I'll keep your cousin in mind, Gladys. But I expect to receive a favorable reply from one of the people we've contacted any day now."

"If you write to Mariah this week she will have time to dispose of her property, resign her present position, and get settled in here before school starts."

Sherman grinned. "You are one determined woman, Gladys Jacobs."

"I am when the situation calls for it," Gladys agreed. "I'm quite certain my cousin would welcome a fresh start, Mr. Butler."

"I have a load of lumber on the wagon, so if you will excuse me. . ."

"How is Lucas and Carrie's house coming along?"

"It will be ready for them to move into by the day of the wedding."

"It doesn't seem possible. Little Carrie getting married, and my Lucille having a baby." Gladys sighed. "Only yesterday they were babies themselves."

"Yes, time passes." Sherman glanced up at the sun. "Speaking of time, I'd better be on my way." Tipping his hat, he took leave of Mrs. Jacobs.

"You contact Mariah this week," she called after him as he swung up on the wagon seat.

Sherman chuckled as he drove away. Gladys Jacobs wouldn't

give him a moment of peace until the teaching position was filled.

The July sun beat down on his shoulders as he turned the matching team of bay workhorses toward the old Nolan place. It didn't seem possible Lucas and Carrie would be married a month from now and she'd be moving away from the Circle C. A lump rose in his throat. She would only be a few miles away, but he was going to miss her something fierce. He wished Caroline could have lived to see the wonderful young woman their headstrong, spoiled little girl had become. She would be mighty proud.

When Caroline died twelve years ago, the pain had been so intense he felt as if his heart was being ripped from his chest. Time had tempered his grief to an occasional dull ache. He still loved her and always would, but more and more she was becoming a faded memory. He lifted his wide-brimmed Stetson and wiped a blue-chambray-clad arm across his damp forehead. Seeing Lucas and Carrie together aroused a longing in him he thought had been buried with Caroline. After all these years alone, Sherman was ready to remarry.

Lord, I'd sure appreciate it if You could send someone special my way. Someone I can love. Someone who will love me in return. A good woman I can share my heart and my life with. Lord, You and me both know I wasn't the husband I should have been to Caroline. But I'm a different man now. If it's Your will, Father, I'd like a second chance.

A drop of sweat trickling down the side of his face reminded him summer was half over. He should be praying for a teacher instead of a wife.

He pulled the piece of paper Gladys Jacobs had given him from his shirt pocket and read aloud the name and address written there. "Miss Mariah Casey, P.O. Box 103, Willow Creek, Ohio." He crumpled the paper in his hand, preparatory to throwing it away. "Regardless of what Gladys says, I doubt Miss Casey would be interested in moving to Cedar Bend."

Of the five letters he sent out in May, he had already received two rejections. Time was running out. "If I don't hear anything in the next week or so, maybe I should contact her."

He smoothed the paper and returned it to his pocket. He'd talk it over with Mac and Cyrus tonight and see what they thought about Gladys's cousin.

Sherman had been a gangly fourteen-year-old orphan when he came in from plowing one day to find two strangers sitting on his front porch. Mac and Cyrus told him they had been with his pa when he fell at Shiloh. He invited them to stay for supper, and they never left. He'd been a restless kid, and a few years after he threw in with Mac and Cyrus, he abandoned the southern Missouri farm where he had been born, and the three of them began to roam. He wasn't overly proud of some of the things he'd done in the following few years. Meeting and marrying Caroline had settled him down considerably and made him think about the future. He and Mac and Cyrus had put together a good-sized herd of cattle and trailed them to Kansas. From that humble beginning, with hard work and perseverance, they had built the Circle C.

A few hours later Sherman sat at the kitchen table with Mac and Cyrus. The three men discussed their day over a final cup of coffee as they had every evening for the past thirty years.

During a lull in the conversation, Sherman mentioned his meeting with Gladys Jacobs that morning. "Seems Gladys has a cousin in Ohio who's a teacher." He chuckled. "She's bound and determined this woman is the answer to our problems. She gave me her name and address and insisted I write to her immediately."

"Wal," Mac said, scratching his bristly chin, "might not be a bad idea to write to this woman."

"Time is runnin' short, Sherm," Cyrus added.

"I still haven't heard from the last three teachers I contacted."

"And you may not." Mac hobbled over to the stove and brought back the coffeepot. After topping off their cups, he returned the pot to the stove and sat back down. "It wouldn't hurt none to get in touch with this woman."

"If I don't hear anything by the end of next week, I've about decided to contact Gladys's cousin."

"In the meantime you might want to write to a few folks back where she lives," Cyrus suggested. "Wouldn't hurt to check and see what folks think of her."

"I reckon I could get some names from Gladys next time I'm in town."

"You best seek the Lord's guidance in this here matter, too," Mac suggested.

"I'll do that." Sherman pushed his chair back from the table. "Tomorrow is a busy day. I think I'll look in on Carrie, then turn in."

☙

Carrie's auburn hair hung in a braid over her shoulder. She looked like a little girl, propped up against the pillows in her long, white nightdress. A pad of paper rested on her bent knees, a stub of a pencil was clenched between her fingers. She had been making innumerable lists since Lucas returned to Cedar Bend two months ago and she began to plan their wedding.

Sherman shuffled a flurry of scribbled pages to one side before sitting down on the edge of the bed. "From the looks of things, you've been busy."

"I had no idea planning a wedding would be so much work." She gathered up the scattered sheets of paper that littered the bed and stacked them on top of the tablet. "But I think I'm almost finished." With a sigh of satisfaction she placed the tablet and pencil on the floor beside her bed. "It is going to be a beautiful wedding, Papa."

He took her hand in his. "I'm sure it will be, little girl." He cleared his throat. "I'm going to miss our nightly talks, Caroline Abigail."

"Me, too, Papa." She looked at him with her mother's dark, Spanish eyes. "But I won't be that far away. We can talk every day."

He wanted to say that it wouldn't be the same. That he would no longer be the most important man in his little girl's life. He wanted to tell her he was a mite jealous of the young man who was taking her away from him. He patted her hand before releasing it.

"Don't look so sad, Papa." Carrie's dimples flashed. "You know Mac's been trying to teach me to cook."

"Mac told me you baked a pie today."

"Did he tell you the crust was so hard we couldn't cut it?" Carrie giggled. "We gave it to Mutt, and he dragged it off and buried it."

"I believe he did mention something about that."

"You know I can't cook, Papa. Poor Mac has just about given up on me." She sighed. "He even told Lucas that if he didn't want to starve until I finally learned how to cook, he was either going to have to learn to do it himself or plan on taking most of his meals here. You will probably get so tired of seeing our faces across the table you'll run us off."

"I can't imagine that ever happening."

"Just wait until we come over dragging five or six grand-children with us." A slight blush tinged her tanned cheeks. "Lucas and I are planning on a large family."

Sherman hadn't thought of his baby with babies of her own. But he decided he rather liked the idea of having young ones around. Being a grandfather might not be half bad.

"Did Hilda Braun talk to you about—" He pulled on his shirt collar. "You know what I mean."

"She did, Papa," Carrie said with a smile.

Sherman breathed a sigh of relief. The Braun family lived on the neighboring ranch. Their oldest daughter, Gretchen, and Carrie had been best friends since they were toddlers. After Caroline died, Carrie spent a lot of time at the Brauns'. He didn't know how he and Mac and Cyrus would have raised his little girl without Hilda Braun's guidance.

"You know Billy and Gretchen are going to stand up with us."

Sherman grinned. "Seems I heard something about that."

"I guess I do go on about wedding plans." Carrie pulled her knees to her chest and wrapped her arms around her legs. "I wish Lucille and Jed could stand up with us, too. But, I suppose since she's expecting, her mother wouldn't think it proper. I asked Joanna Brady to sing, but we haven't chosen the songs yet. What did they sing at your wedding, Papa?"

Sherman thought back to that long-ago day and shook his head. "I haven't the slightest idea, little girl. Something in Spanish, I think. I was so nervous I don't remember anything clearly except kissing your mama."

"That's so sweet, Papa." Carrie rested her chin on her knees. "I miss her so much sometimes. Do you think she knows about Lucas?"

"I couldn't say, Carrie."

"She would love him, wouldn't she?"

"She was fond of him when he was a young boy. I'm certain he would meet with her approval."

"I think she would be pleased that we're building our house on the foundation of Lucas's boyhood home, don't you?"

"I think she would."

"Our house is coming along really well, don't you think?"

"I do." Sherman shifted a bit on the bed. "I saw Gladys Jacobs this morning when I went into town for supplies."

Carrie wrinkled her nose. "What did she have to say?"

"Now, Carrie, Mrs. Jacobs means well." Sherman touched a finger to the tip of Carrie's nose.

"You know that I love Mrs. Jacobs." Carrie grinned. "She spent years trying to transform me into a proper young lady. Aggravated me to no end. Remember the sidesaddle, Papa? It was her final effort. After that failed she gave up on me."

"Not quite." Sherman grinned. "There was still the episode with the corset."

"She won that one." Carrie giggled. "Well, sort of. I wear a corset if I have to, but I still reserve the right to despise them."

"Mrs. Jacobs loves you, Carrie." Sherman gave the long auburn braid a gentle yank.

"I know she does, Papa." Carrie sighed. "Now that I'm older I realize everything she did was out of love. Love for me, but especially love for Mama. She tried to take Mama's place, but she couldn't. No one could ever take her place, right, Papa?"

"No," Sherman agreed. "No one could ever take Caroline's place."

"One time when I was about twelve, Mrs. Jacobs told me it would be nice if you remarried." Carrie's softly rounded chin took on a determined tilt. "I set her straight on that." She leaned forward and wrapped her arms around Sherman's neck. "I told her you were perfectly happy as you were."

Sherman savored the clean smell of her hair as he held her close. His life was going to be so empty without her.

She released him and leaned back against the pillows. "What did Mrs. Jacobs have to say?"

"Well. . ." Sherman cleared his throat and blinked back a sheen of wetness from his eyes. "She suggested I write to her cousin and offer her the teaching position."

"The old-maid schoolteacher in Ohio?"

"What do you know about Gladys's cousin?"

"Not much." Carrie frowned in concentration. "I think her father died when she was about my age. Ever since then she has taught school and taken care of her mother. Lucille says she is like Cinderella, except she isn't beautiful, and there will never be a handsome prince to rescue her from a life of dreary servitude."

Sherman stifled a chuckle. Lucille was imaginative and melodramatic. He'd learned long ago to take what she said with a grain of salt.

"Before Lucille met Jed, she said she was going to end up like her cousin. 'This is how I shall live, and this is how I shall die,' she always said. 'An old maid schoolteacher unsullied by the hand of man, just like Cousin Mariah.'"

Sherman stood. "Well, I believe I shall turn in." He leaned over to kiss Carrie's cheek. "Good night, little girl. Sweet dreams."

"Good night, Papa." Carrie pulled the sheet up to her chin as he walked to the door. "I think you should write to Mrs. Jacobs's cousin."

Sherman hesitated, his hand on the doorknob. "Why is that?"

"You know how teachers stay about a year then get married?" Carrie sat up. "I was just thinking. Mrs. Jacobs's cousin is close to forty. No one will want to marry an old maid like her. She could probably teach for years and years. Just think of all the trouble it would save the school board if they didn't have to search for a new teacher every year."

"Maybe you're right." Sherman tried to recall being so young that forty seemed old. "I'll certainly give it some thought."

Carrie turned out the lamp before snuggling down on her pillow. "I love you, Papa."

"Love you, too." Sherman closed the door behind him and turned his steps toward his own bed.

two

Mariah woke early on the morning of her thirty-sixth birthday. Swinging her feet over the edge of the bed, she sat up. The heat was oppressive in the closed room. Her high-necked gown, worn thin, clung to her back. Tendrils of dark hair that escaped her thick, waist-length braid were plastered to her temples. She stood, crossed the room, and pulled back the heavy drapes. It didn't help much. The air was heavy with humidity.

A half hour later, freshly bathed and dressed in lightweight, white knit drawers and a low-necked, sleeveless summer vest, Mariah stood before her bedroom mirror and loosened her braid. Her lustrous, dark hair and smooth, flawless skin were the only features she had inherited from her dainty, feminine mother. Her sapphire blue eyes and lanky frame came from her father. Almost six feet tall, she was what most people called *plain*.

Even now on the brink of middle age, she blushed at the memory of the beauty cream she had sneaked into her room when she was sixteen. She still recalled word for word the ad that beguiled her: *"If nature has not favored you with that greatest charm and beauty, send for our product and you will be pleased over the result of a few weeks' time. Will make any lady beautiful as a princess."*

It took her months to save the necessary dollar and a half. After six months of faithful and unproductive use, her mother found the cream and threw it away. The harangue that followed still made Mariah's heart ache.

"You are a fool, Mariah," Mother scolded. "If it was meant

for you to be beautiful, you would have been born that way. You were a long, scrawny, homely baby. I was ashamed to have my friends see you when you were a newborn, and time has done nothing to improve your appearance."

Mariah cried herself to sleep that night, not because Mother slapped her and threw away the beauty cream, but because she knew her mother didn't love her.

She pulled the brush through her hair a final time. The light caught on a single strand of silver. Mariah hesitated a moment before slicking the wavy tresses back and securing them in a large, no-nonsense bun on the back of her head. Crossing the room, she opened the door of the massive wardrobe. She was too tall for ready-made and too impoverished to pay a dressmaker, so necessity dictated that she make her own clothes. Fortunately she was as efficient at the sewing machine as she was in the classroom. She perused the neat row of white shirtwaists and dark-colored skirts before choosing a faded calico housedress. This morning she would work in her garden.

Fully dressed, sitting alone at the oak kitchen table, she bowed her head and whispered a prayer before eating her customary breakfast: an egg boiled for precisely three minutes, a thick slice of homemade bread spread with jam, and one cup of hot tea.

After her few dishes were washed, dried, and put away, she sat in the rocking chair in the kitchen. Taking her Bible from the small chair-side table, she opened the worn leather cover. A slip of paper listed the number of chapters to be read each day in order to complete the Bible in one year. This morning she dutifully read the prescribed chapters in Jeremiah. With the completion of the final verse, she carefully placed the ribbon marker between the pages and closed her Bible.

On her knees in front of the rocking chair, she tried to pray but found it impossible to stay focused. In the first months following her mother's death, Mariah prayed daily for her life to be different. An excellent cook, she dreamed of having friends over to share Sunday dinner. She fantasized about a special woman friend. Someone she could share confidences with. God hadn't answered her prayers. Why had she expected Him to? When she was small, she prayed for a baby brother or sister. When she was older, she prayed for a husband and children. Always she pleaded with God to send her someone to love. God sat on His throne and turned a deaf ear to her entreaties.

When she stood, her sleeve brushed against a letter lying on the table. Her only cousin's most recent correspondence came yesterday, but she hadn't felt like reading Gladys's maternal ramblings about her two daughters and their domestic bliss. Now, as she picked up the thick packet, she discovered a second slim envelope beneath.

Mariah put on gold-rimmed reading glasses and sat down in the rocking chair. She first skimmed through the unexpected letter and then read it thoroughly. When she finished, she leaned back in her chair. Sherman Butler, president of the school board in Cedar Bend, Kansas, was offering her a teaching position. Gladys must have given Mr. Butler her address. She laid the letter to one side and opened her cousin's letter.

Gladys began with news of her family. Her younger daughter, Lucille, was expecting her first child any day. Mariah couldn't believe Lucille had been married long enough to be a mother, but after counting off the months on her fingers, she realized her young cousin had married well over a year ago. Time seemed to pass so quickly sometimes.

Gladys also wrote at length about a friend of Lucille's named Carrie Butler and her upcoming wedding. Carrie was the teacher she would be replacing if she accepted the position.

"You need to be with family, Mariah," Gladys wrote. "I know this is short notice, but please say you will come."

She read Mr. Butler's letter a third time. The salary he quoted was more than generous. She had never been more than ten miles outside the city limits of Willow Creek. Could this job offer be the beginning of the new life she longed for?

The clock in the parlor chimed six times, reminding Mariah there was work to be done. She laid Sherman Butler's letter on the table with her cousin's letter. In the serenity of her garden she would consider Mr. Butler's offer.

Mariah spent the morning working with her flowers. The months following her mother's death had been as lonely as the years preceding it. Women her age were busy with husbands and children. Those younger pursued their own interests, mainly finding the perfect man and becoming wives and mothers. It seemed no one had time for a lonely spinster.

Tears lingered just below the surface, but she refused to surrender to self-pity. In the year following her twenty-fifth birthday, when she accepted her spinsterhood as a permanent state, she shed her final tears. After all, what had those tears accomplished?

She gave a vicious yank at a stubborn weed. This morning when she discovered the strand of silver in her dark hair, she had considered yanking it out. "Vanity," she murmured as she pulled another recalcitrant weed.

Her mother had been vain. So vain she had let an all but invisible scar and a slight limp cut her off from the world. After the accident, Mother drew the heavy drapes, took down the mirrors, and cloistered herself in the gloomy house. Except for school, church, and occasional trips for food, in the dark months while her gardens slept beneath a thick blanket of snow, Mariah was forced to share her mother's prison.

Mother was gone, but the prison remained. Curly tendrils escaped Mariah's severe hairdo and plastered to her temples. She blotted the sweat from her face with a gloved hand. It was time to go inside. Still kneeling amidst the blossoms, she took a moment to consider the question that had been on her mind since she read Mr. Butler's letter. *Should I go to Kansas?*

She stood and surveyed her flowers. Eighteen years ago she had begun to cultivate her gardens and dream of a handsome prince on a prancing steed who would rescue her from a dreary life of loneliness. The gardens flourished until the yard of the former parsonage became a showplace. The prince, however, never appeared. Eleven years ago Mariah quit looking for him.

Should I go to Kansas? The tall hollyhocks growing against the fence behind her vegetable garden stirred gently in the faint breeze. A bee gathered nectar from the zinnias at her feet. As she walked to the porch, the roses nestled by the back steps perfumed the air. She stooped to breathe in the fragrance of the yellow blossoms before continuing up the steps. Sitting in a wicker rocker, screened from view by a lattice weighed down with morning glory vines, Mariah removed her gloves, then bent to unlace her shoes. Should she go to Kansas? She closed her eyes and rested her forehead against her knees.

She had been a young girl when the Jacobs left Ohio, but she remembered their kindness to her. Gladys had given her a fluffy yellow kitten the day they left. "Something of your own you can love and care for," Cousin Gladys whispered in her ear when she hugged her a final time. The Jacobs were scarcely out of sight when Mother took the kitten from her. Mariah blinked back scalding tears.

Why shouldn't she go to Kansas? Willow Creek held nothing but unpleasant memories. In Kansas she would be close to the only family she had left. If she remained in Willow Creek, when at last she was laid to rest in the churchyard beside her parents, there would be no family to mourn her passing. No one, except for a few former students perhaps, to remember her with fondness.

The job offer from Kansas was her means of escape. A chance for the new beginning she had prayed for. She pulled off her shoes and stood. For a moment she scanned the yard with its brilliant display of color; then she squared her shoulders.

There would be flowers in Cedar Bend. And maybe. . .just maybe. . . *Oh, please, Lord, let there be someone I can love.*

three

Mariah closed her book and tucked it and her glasses into the large, leather Gladstone bag that had belonged to her father. Outside the coach window, undulating fields of grass, scorched golden by the early September heat, stretched as far as she could see.

Mariah leaned her head against the high back of the seat and closed her eyes. Today she would leave the train and board a stagecoach for the final miles of her journey. She had telegraphed Cousin Gladys from the last stop informing her of the stage's approximate arrival time. Would she be there to meet her?

Her seatmate—a plump, grandmotherly woman named Mrs. Sellers—woke with a start. "I musta dozed off." She yawned. "Lands sakes, seems as if I can't set down without noddin' off. I'd reckon I'm gettin' old. Where'd you tell me you was goin' to, dear?"

Mariah opened her eyes and turned her head toward Mrs. Sellers. "I didn't say."

The other woman laughed. "I'd reckon you didn't. So where are you goin'? Not that it's any of my business. I'd reckon I'm just an old busybody."

Mrs. Sellers *was* a busybody. Since she boarded the train yesterday evening she'd bombarded Mariah with an endless stream of questions. Not that she answered any more of them than civility demanded. Mariah didn't make a habit of sharing her personal affairs with anyone, least of all a stranger on a train.

"I'm goin' to stay with my daughter fer a few months."

The older woman chattered on, her question about Mariah's destination seemingly forgotten. "She's feelin' poorly, you know. Not that Carl ain't a big help. It's jist that the poor man can't be expected to work all day then come home to take care of five youngsters, you know. Soon's the new baby comes and Sally's back on her feet, I'll be goin' home." A cloud passed over her cheerful face. "Not that there's much to go home to since my Abner passed away last year, you know. After forty years of havin' him always there it's mighty hard to be alone." She sighed; then her face brightened. "Of course, I've got a wonderful church family. You seen some of 'em when I got on the train. They insisted on comin' to see me off. The Lord surely has been good to me."

Mariah's minister and his wife were the only ones standing on the platform when she boarded the train. She turned to look out the window. Pastor Billings and his wife had been there out of duty, not because they cared about her. Even though he took her father's place in the pulpit almost eighteen years ago, he scarcely knew her. The thought brought tears to her eyes, which she quickly blinked away. She would not allow herself to indulge in self-pity.

Mrs. Sellers's soft elbow in her ribs interrupted her thoughts. "We're almost there, dear."

❧

Two hours later Mariah traveled over the gently rolling prairie in a stagecoach. Clouds of dust thrown up by the horses' hooves drifted past the open window. She had given up trying to brush away the fine powder that settled on her black suit.

A husky man occupied the seat facing her. The other two passengers—boys in their late teens—had climbed on top with the driver. The man introduced himself as Karl Braun, then tipped his hat over his eyes. Moments later roof-raising snores began to emanate from his open mouth.

Mariah reached up to adjust her hat, at the same time

discreetly removing a six-inch hat pin. If the man attempted anything improper, she would be prepared to defend herself.

Mariah took a book from her bag and settled down to do some reading. She had read *Little Women* countless times but still loved the story. An hour later she sighed as she turned the final page and closed the cover. She could only imagine having a mother like the March sisters. A mother who loved her children even if they weren't pretty.

The man stirred and thumbed his hat off his eyes. "You from back East?"

"I'm from Ohio," she replied, her hand tightening on the hat pin now concealed beneath the folds of her skirt.

"Next stop's about a mile ahead." The man put a hand to the back of his neck and rolled his head. "Got a crick in my neck," he explained. "That your stop? Cedar Bend?"

"Yes." Mariah shifted a little on the unyielding seat in a futile effort to relieve the kinks in her aching back.

"I'd reckon you're gonna be our new schoolteacher. I'm on the school board. I knew Mr. Butler had contacted you, but I've been out of town on business the last three weeks and didn't know if you'd accepted the job. You are Gladys Jacobs's cousin?"

Mariah realized Mr. Braun was waiting for her to introduce herself. She made it a policy not to converse with strangers—especially men—but the gentleman across from her seemed harmless enough. Besides, in a manner of speaking, he was her employer. She slipped the hat pin back in her hat and extended her right hand. "My name is Mariah Casey, Mr. Braun. My father and Gladys's father were brothers."

The man's hand was calloused, the handshake firm and brief. "I see a family resemblance. You put me in mind of Lucille."

"I have never met my cousin's younger daughter, and Clara, her eldest, was barely five years old when they left Ohio."

"We've had quite a time keeping a teacher. Last two didn't

last no time 'til they got married. I'd reckon you gotta expect that with young girls. Especially the pretty ones." The man settled back in the seat. "I'm glad you accepted the job. Looking for a new teacher every year was startin' to get a mite burdensome."

Mariah, feeling the color rising in her face, turned her head to look out the window.

"That's Sherman Butler's land," the man observed. "He owns a big hunk of Kansas. His little girl, Carrie, was the teacher in Cedar Bend last year, but she got married a month ago. Carrie and my oldest girl, Gretchen, have been best friends since they were knee-high to a grasshopper. She's a pretty little thing, Carrie is. Sweet, too. You might think being raised without a mother she'd be a regular little terror, but she's not."

Mariah found herself listening with interest. After all, the people he was talking about were going to be her neighbors, and she hoped her friends.

"Of course I give my Hilda credit for most of that. After her Mama died, Carrie spent a lot of time at our place. We have the ranch next to the Circle C."

"Do you have children that will be attending school, Mr. Braun?"

The man's hearty laugh brought an answering smile to Mariah's lips. "We have ten. There is Gretchen, our firstborn. She's married now. James just turned eighteen, and Tad is sixteen. They're the two riding topside. Katy is almost fifteen. The four oldest are through with school. Jay is almost fourteen; he will be in his final year. Then there is"—he counted off on his fingers—"Michael, Hugh, Little Karl, Abigail, and Paul. The two youngest won't go this year. Little Karl—we call him L. K.—is barely six. Hilda was thinking about holding him back a year, but he's been begging to go to school. She finally decided to let him go."

"I'm sure with so many older brothers to look after him he will do fine."

"They're good boys, Miss Casey. If any of them gives you the slightest bit of trouble, let me know."

"I have taught for eighteen years, Mr. Braun. I don't anticipate trouble."

"The kids in Cedar Bend have been raised to respect their elders, Miss Casey. I doubt if you'll have trouble with them. Still, boys can be high-spirited and mischievous. If you have a problem with any of the youngsters, mine or anyone else's, let one of the school board members know. We'll take care of it."

Mariah nodded, then turned her attention to brushing the dust from her jacket.

A few minutes later Karl Braun gave Mariah a hand down from the stagecoach. A slight woman with graying hair hurried up to her. "Mariah Casey, it has been twenty-five years, but I would know you anywhere."

Not knowing how to respond when the older woman embraced her, Mariah stood stiffly until her cousin's arms dropped away and she stepped back.

"You look very much like your father." A slender, slightly stoop-shouldered man moved to Gladys's side. "You remember my Nels?"

"Yes, of course," Mariah murmured, though in truth she remembered only their kindness to her.

"We're happy to have you with us, Mariah." Nels smiled and patted her arm.

Mariah nodded. "I am happy to be here."

"I'll collect your bags while you two women get re-acquainted." Karl Braun walked to the small pile of luggage his sons were stacking beside the coach. "You boys load Miss Casey's things into Mr. Jacobs's buggy," he ordered.

While the boys made short work of loading the luggage, Gladys regaled Mariah with stories of her two daughters and their families. Mariah noticed Karl Braun walk over to a young woman standing on the boardwalk. She attempted to listen to her cousin, but her attention was on the young woman. She was tall and slender, with auburn hair in a thick braid that reached her waist. A wide-brimmed hat shaded her face, hiding it from view. Although she wasn't wearing men's clothing, she wasn't dressed like a lady, either. Her white shirt had full sleeves gathered into wide cuffs at the wrist. The skirt she wore was green and divided. Not exactly trousers, but close enough, it ended halfway between her knees and ankles. Even though the girl's tight-fitting boots covered her legs, Mariah thought the outfit unbecoming a lady.

A buckboard moved slowly down the street and stopped behind the stage. The Brauns climbed in with the lanky young driver. The buckboard made a U-turn in the middle of the street and headed back the way it had come.

"That was Billy Racine, Karl and Hilda Braun's new son-in-law," Gladys said, interrupting her own account of Lucille's new baby boy. "Oh, dear, in all the excitement I almost forgot Carrie." She took Mariah's arm and led her to the young woman. "Carrie Nolan, I would like to introduce you to my cousin Mariah Casey."

"I have been looking forward to meeting you, Miss Casey." The girl lifted her head, and Mariah found herself looking into the most beautiful face she had ever seen.

"Yes." Mariah felt awkward, tongue-tied, and homelier than usual. "Well, I am happy to be here."

"Papa is away on business, so he appointed me to help you get settled in." Her laugh was young, carefree, and bubbly. "You said in your letter that you would like a house of your own?"

"Nonsense," Gladys said. "Mariah will be staying with us."

"No, Cousin Gladys. It would be an imposition for you and Cousin Nels. Besides I have lived alone for some time, and I cherish my privacy."

"You are family, Mariah. We would love to have you."

"Mr. Butler informed me in his letter that the school provides a house. I will stay with you until my things arrive, Cousin Gladys. Then I will move into that house." When her cousin began to protest, Mariah shook her head. "Please, this is one thing I am adamant about. I will feel more comfortable surrounded by my own things."

"Would it be all right if I picked you up at the Jacobs's tomorrow morning?" Carrie asked. "I could show you the school. Also, Papa thought you would like to see the house. Would nine thirty be all right with you?"

"Yes. That would be fine."

"Good." Carrie smiled. "I better be getting home. Lucas will be starved."

Gladys placed her hand on Carrie's arm. "Have you tried any of the recipes I gave you?"

"A couple, Mrs. Jacobs. But mostly we eat at Papa's." Her happy laugh rang out. "I don't want to poison Lucas. Besides Mac loves to have us. I'll see you tomorrow, Miss Casey."

The girl untied a bay mare from the hitching rail, placed a small, boot-clad foot in the stirrup, and swung into the saddle. She gave a final wave before turning the horse. Mariah watched in disbelief as she galloped down the street. Astride!

Gladys seemed not to notice the Nolan woman's unconventional behavior. "Carrie is quite a girl. Those three men spoiled her rotten after her mother died." Gladys beamed. "Hilda Braun and I tried to advise her, not that we could ever take Caroline's place. Still, Carrie is a sweet girl. She's becoming quite a proper young lady, too. I like to think I'm partly responsible for that."

Mariah was sure there were many words one could use to describe Carrie Nolan, but in her opinion *proper* and *lady* were not on the list.

four

At 9:25 Mariah walked to the edge of the porch and looked up and down the street. Not seeing an approaching conveyance of any sort, she sat down on the porch swing. Five minutes later she heard the clock in Cousin Gladys's parlor strike the half hour. After another quick check up and down the street, she returned to the swing.

A few minutes later her cousin joined her. "Carrie will be here by ten," Gladys said.

"She told me nine thirty."

"Well, things come up. You know how it is."

"No, I do not know how it is. Nine thirty means half past nine to me." Mariah found tardiness intolerable.

Gladys lingered for a few minutes chatting—mostly about Lucille and her new baby—before excusing herself and going back inside.

The clock in the parlor was striking ten when Carrie arrived. Mariah hurried down the walk and climbed into the buggy.

"Sorry to be late." Carrie's smile was dazzling. "We overslept. Then I had to see my husband off. I was sure you would understand."

"I understand, Mrs. Nolan." A quick glance assured Mariah that her companion was as perfect of face and form as she had thought her on their first meeting. This morning, clad in a blue-flowered dress and a white straw bonnet, the young woman was a picture of femininity. "However," Mariah continued, turning her gaze to the street ahead of them, "I have always prided myself on being a quarter hour early to any

29

appointment. I have always believed that lack of punctuality indicates a lack of virtue."

She could feel Carrie's eyes on her. Words of apology for her harshness were on her lips when the girl giggled. "You sound like Mac. He always says, 'Little lady, you'll be late fer yer own funeral.' I apologize for my tardiness, Miss Casey. Please forgive me."

Mariah fidgeted with the clasp on her purse before taking a deep breath. "Your apology is accepted."

"Good. Now, which would you like to see first? The school? Or the house?"

"The school. Most assuredly, the school."

While Carrie secured the lines to the hitching rail, Mariah stood looking up at the freshly painted, white, rectangular frame building. The two windows that flanked the front door glistened, newly washed and spot free. "It appears well kept," she said.

"We are proud of our school." Carrie moved to enter the building.

Mariah followed Carrie up the three shallow steps and across the porch to the front door. "It isn't locked?" she asked, when Carrie turned the knob and swung the door inward.

"No one ever bothers anything." Carrie stood aside for Mariah to enter.

The room was not much larger than her second grade classroom in Ohio. The south wall contained a row of sparkling windows. The desks, though showing signs of wear, were polished to a soft shine.

Their heels clicked on the oiled wooden floor as they walked to the front of the room. Mariah stepped behind the battered desk with the blackboard to her back and rows of desks before her. There were six rows of desks with eight desks in a row. The smallest desks were next to the window, and they gradually increased in size to the largest ones against the windowless north wall. *Forty-eight children of different ages and different grade levels.* Uncertainty tempered Mariah's anticipation. *How will I ever competently teach so many children?* Mariah sat down in the chair and folded her hands on top of the desk.

"I know it looks rather daunting." Carrie stood beside the desk. "I was terrified the first time I sat behind that desk." She walked over to the first row of desks. "My second graders sat here. My third in the next row, and so on." She turned to two low tables surrounded by miniature chairs on Mariah's right. "My little first graders sat at these tables where I could keep an eye on them." She rested her hand on the back of one of the chairs and looked out over the empty classroom. "I love all of them, and I am going to miss them."

Mariah cleared her throat. "I have always made it a policy not to become attached to my pupils."

Carrie looked at her with wide eyes. "How can you not? Especially the little ones. They are so precious and so eager to learn."

"I have taught for eighteen years, Mrs. Nolan." She rose from the desk and walked to the bookshelves on the north wall. "In my experience it is better for all concerned if one maintains a distance from the children." She ran a long, slender finger down the spine of a book. "I see you have an excellent selection of reading material."

"We are not illiterate, Miss Casey."

She turned to face the young woman. "I never said you were, Mrs. Nolan. You misunderstood."

Carrie turned away. "If you are through here, I'll take you to see the house."

"Yes, I think I have seen enough." Mariah pushed the chair under the desk. "One more thing, Mrs. Nolan. The door is to be locked when school is not in session. I will require a key. No one else is to have access to the building, except the president of the school board, of course."

As she gathered her purse and gloves from the desk, Mariah saw the young woman roll her eyes. "I'll make it a priority to deliver your message to my father as soon as possible." Carrie turned and swept out of the room.

When Mariah climbed into the buggy, she ventured, "If it is permissible, I'll come back every day this week to prepare my lesson plans."

Carrie picked up the reins. "Do as you please, Miss Casey. With your vast experience I'm quite sure you know more than I what is necessary."

As they rode silently away from the school, Mariah sat stiffly beside Carrie. She had been intimidated by the young woman's looks from the moment she met her. As always when she felt threatened she retreated behind a screen of false superiority. She had been hateful to Carrie Nolan, and she was ashamed of her actions. She wanted to apologize, but the words wouldn't come. Instead she prayed inwardly, *Dear Lord, I am so sorry for my actions. I didn't mean the things I said to Mrs. Nolan. You know how desperately I wish to change. To become a woman who is worthy of friendship. Help me to control my tongue in the future.*

❧

Mariah fell in love with the white frame house with the yellow roses blooming beside the front gate as soon as she saw it. A leisurely walk through the five large rooms confirmed her first impression.

"I want to buy this house," she said.

"There is no need for that. The school board furnishes the house for you rent free."

"I would prefer not to rent, Mrs. Nolan. Who owns it? I'll talk to him or her personally."

"I believe Eli Smith at the bank is the owner, but it isn't for sale."

"Nonsense." Mariah heard the harshness in her own voice

and attempted to amend it. "In any case it won't hurt to ask. If you will direct me to the bank—"

"I'll drive you. But this house is not for sale."

❧

On Saturday, Sherman Butler returned from his business trip to Texas. That evening he sat down to supper with his two partners and his son-in-law and daughter. After they had thoroughly discussed his trip, Sherman turned to Carrie. "What did you think of the new teacher, little girl?"

Lucas laughed as he reached for the green beans. "I made the mistake of asking that question, Sherm. Prepare for an earful."

"Wait until you meet her, Pa." Carrie smirked at her husband.

"She had excellent references." Sherman frowned. "What's wrong with her, Carrie?"

"Everything. When I went to the Jacobs's to pick her up the morning after her arrival and take her to visit the school, the first thing she did was scold me for being late."

Mac chuckled. "How late was you, little lady?"

"Only thirty minutes, and I had a good reason, too."

"I allus did say if you was a half hour late you was early," the little man teased.

"Anyway," Carrie continued, choosing to ignore Mac's comment, "she was sitting on the porch swing looking like she was about to explode. I barely got the buggy stopped before she marched down the walk and climbed in. I apologized for being late. Do you know what she said? Well, do you?"

"I'd reckon since we wasn't there, young 'un, we couldn't know what she said."

"I know what she said, Cyrus." Lucas winked at the Circle C foreman. "But I can't tell this story with the same flair as my wife." He patted Carrie's clenched fist. "You tell them, sugar."

"She said that lack of punctuality indicated a lack of virtue. I didn't get angry. I wanted to, but I didn't. You would have been proud of me. That wasn't the worst, though. While I was showing her the school she said a teacher should maintain distance from her pupils. Can you imagine? I had to bite my tongue to keep from telling her what I thought of her."

"Now, little lady," Mac said, "you don't know this woman. Ain't I always told you, you cain't tell what's in a package by lookin' at the wrappin'?"

"I know what's in this package," Carrie said. "A hateful old maid with no heart. Oh, I almost forgot. Miss Casey said for you to have two keys made so she can lock the school when she's not there. The only other person who gets a key is you, Papa. Can you imagine that?"

"Simmer down now, young 'un. The lady more'n likely ain't never lived in a little town like Cedar Bend. She ain't used to trustin' her neighbors," Cyrus said. "Mac's right, much as I hate to agree with the old coot. You don't know the teacher well enough to pass judgment. I 'spect she feels a mite strange here. She'll probably be right nice once you get to know her."

"Wait until you meet her," Carrie grumbled. "You'll see."

"Did she like Eli Smith's house all right?" Sherman asked.

"She must have." Carrie snorted. "She bought it."

"I didn't realize it was for sale."

"Neither did Eli until Miss Casey walked into his office. She told him she had the money from the sale of her house in Ohio, and since Cedar Bend was going to be her home from this day forth, she wanted a place she could call her own. She frightened the poor man out of his wits. Or, I suppose I should say, out of his property."

Sherman chuckled. "Knowing Eli, I'm sure he didn't get hurt in the transaction."

"I guess not," Carrie agreed grudgingly. "But I still don't like her ways."

❧

Sherman rolled over for the fifth time. What if they had made a mistake hiring Mariah Casey sight unseen? He punched the pillow, trying to mold it into a more accommodating shape. What had the letters of recommendation actually said? "Miss Casey is dependable. Reliable. Competent. Of high moral character." Even though she had been living among these people her entire life, they could have been writing about a stranger.

He would meet Miss Casey tomorrow after church. He sighed deeply and rolled over again. Come morning he would know if the new teacher was as bad as Carrie said.

five

Mariah sat beside her cousin, her eyes fixed on the plump young woman standing at the front of the small church. "If you will turn in your hymnals to page 219, we will sing 'Near the Cross.'"

"The song leader is Joanna Brady," Gladys whispered to Mariah. "Her father is our doctor."

All around her, voices raised in praise. Mariah held the hymnal in front of her, silently mouthing the words of the beautiful old hymn. When she was small she loved to sing. Then one day Mother told her she sounded like an old crow in the corn patch, and the music inside Mariah died. The memory of that day, even though it had been almost thirty years ago, brought back a pain that stabbed through her like a knife.

As the congregation sang the final chorus, Carrie Nolan swept down the center aisle followed by a tall, broad-shouldered man. The young couple slid into the second pew from the front next to a white-haired gentleman that Mariah assumed was Mrs. Nolan's father. She frowned at the back of Carrie's head. If she didn't respect the Lord enough to arrive on time, she should have the decency to sit in the rear of the church where her entry didn't create a disturbance. Mariah realized that she was passing judgment on young Mrs. Nolan again and quickly asked the Lord to help her overcome her unkind thoughts.

After his sermon, the pastor made a few announcements concerning upcoming events. "In conclusion," he said, "I would like to introduce a special guest. Miss Casey, will you please stand?"

It took the sharp jab of Gladys's elbow in her ribs to bring her slowly to her feet.

"Miss Casey is our new teacher." The pastor smiled. "As you all know, a carry-in dinner is being held at the Cattlemen's Association building today in her honor. The ladies of Cedar Bend have prepared a bountiful repast as always. You will have an opportunity to enjoy some of the best food in the state at the same time you are making the acquaintance of our new teacher. Welcome to Cedar Bend, Miss Casey."

A round of applause brought a rush of color to Mariah's face. She knew they expected her to say something. The most she could manage was a murmured "Thank you" before resuming her seat.

"Why didn't you tell me about the dinner?" she whispered to her cousin.

"It was to be a surprise." Gladys smiled and patted her arm as they rose for the final song.

～

Within minutes of their arrival at the Cattlemen's Association, Gladys had introduced Mariah to so many people her mind whirled. How would she ever remember so many faces and the names that went with them?

"Mariah, this is Joanna Brady," Gladys said. "You remember, she is our song leader."

"Of course," Mariah replied. "You have a lovely voice, Miss Brady."

"Thank you." The young woman smiled. "Miss Casey, may I introduce my father, Dr. Tom Brady?"

A lanky man moved to Joanna's side. "Dr. Brady is a member of the school board," Gladys said.

"Welcome to Cedar Bend, Miss Casey. I hope you will be happy here."

"I'm sure I will." There was a strong resemblance between the doctor and his daughter. They were both olive-skinned with dark hair and gentle, brown eyes. But, while he was tall and angular, Joanna was short and softly rounded.

"Say, Sherm just walked in the door." Tom Brady motioned to someone behind Mariah. "He's coming over. You haven't met Sherman Butler yet, have you?"

"I believe I saw him in church." When Mariah turned, she expected to see the silver-haired man Carrie Nolan had sat beside. Instead she found herself being introduced to a tall, handsome man with thick, curly, auburn hair and a well-groomed mustache. He didn't appear to be much older than herself. "Mr. Sherman Butler, may I introduce Miss Mariah Casey, our new teacher?"

"Miss Casey, welcome to Cedar Bend." His handshake was firm. "My daughter tells me you bought a house."

Mariah nodded. "It seemed a wise investment with the state of the economy and so many banks back East failing."

"I think you made a wise choice. One never knows what will happen in times like these. I hope President Cleveland is able to get a handle on things and this depression doesn't last too long."

"Papa, I've been looking for you." Carrie Nolan linked her arm through her father's. "Hello, Miss Casey. I should imagine you are prepared for tomorrow."

"It took the better part of the week," she said, "to put things in their proper order."

"I thought everything was in order."

Mariah looked into Carrie's beautiful face and read the disdain in her dark eyes. "Orderly, yes, of course, but not conducive to my methods of teaching."

"Well, I suppose you would know more about that than I." Carrie smiled sweetly. "After all, you were teaching before I was born." She tugged gently on her father's arm. "They're ready to begin, Papa. Come sit with us."

Mariah knew she had further alienated Mrs. Nolan with

her sharp tongue. Why must she always be on the defensive? Carrie Nolan could no more help being beautiful than *she* could help being plain.

"I'm happy you are here, Miss Casey." The big man smiled as Carrie led him away.

"Would you sit with my father and me, Miss Casey?" Joanna Brady asked.

She turned to the nonthreatening young woman. "Yes. Thank you, Miss Brady."

Her smile lit up her sweet face. "Please call me Joanna."

❧

"See what I meant about her?" Carrie slid into the chair beside her husband. "There was nothing wrong with my schoolroom."

Her father took the chair beside her. "Everyone has different ideas on how things should be done, little girl. I wouldn't judge Miss Casey too harshly."

They stood to pray before Carrie had a chance to reply.

While they ate, Sherman had ample opportunity to observe the teacher seated across the room. Several people stopped by the table to speak to her. Though she replied, there was nothing in her manner to encourage them to linger, and they quickly moved on. Was she shy or, as Carrie insisted, cold and hateful?

As soon as they finished eating, people began to circulate and gather in small groups to visit. Sherman saw Felicia Wainwright sweep through the door with two small girls. Her daughter, Callista, was dressed like a little princess in white ruffles with pink bows in her blond hair. Hope, her orphaned niece, wore an ill-fitting dress that looked as though it had been made from a flowered feed sack. The woman scanned the room until her sharp eyes came to rest on Mariah Casey. The two girls in tow, she bore down on the teacher.

Sherman knew that Felicia Wainwright had brought Carrie to tears on more than one occasion. He wondered how Miss Casey would handle the woman's demands.

⊱

"Excuse me. I am Mrs. Felicia Wainwright. Are you the new teacher?"

With a glance, Mariah took in the stout woman's elaborately styled blond hair and haughty expression. "Yes, I am Mariah Casey."

"My daughter will be in your second grade class this year." She rested a hand on the head of a miniature version of herself. "This is my darling Callista. Callista, precious, this is Miss Casey. She will be your teacher. Say hello to Miss Casey, dear."

The pudgy child stared silently at Mariah.

"Callista is very bright. You shan't have a bit of trouble with her." She laid hold of the smaller girl's arm and urged her forward. "However, I would like a few words with you about my niece. Callista, dear, I saw some of your little friends outside. Why don't you go play with them while I speak with Miss Casey?"

"I have to leave," Callista spoke in a high-pitched whine, "because she doesn't want me to hear what she has to say about Hope. Hope can stay because she's a dummy."

Mariah saw the same pain in the tiny girl's eyes she had seen reflected in her own mirror after one of her mother's barbed comments. Her heart ached for the defenseless child. "Go play with the other children, Callista."

Callista's eyes widened. Her lower lip trembled ever so slightly. "Now!" Mariah insisted. With a frightened glance the child dashed away.

"Don't get dirty, precious," her mother called after her. "I suppose I should apologize for my daughter." She smiled at Mariah. "But she is only a child. She hasn't yet learned to control her tongue."

Mariah frowned. "Children learn from the example that is set before them."

"Callista meant no harm." The woman managed a weak

laugh. "After all, we have all heard the old saying, 'Sticks and stones may break my bones, but names will never hurt me.'"

"That is an erroneous saying, Mrs. Wainwright. Names break hearts and destroy spirits. I do not allow any child in my classroom to be abused, either verbally or physically."

"What Callista said to Hope couldn't possibly hurt her. My niece is deaf."

Mariah looked at the beautiful little girl. "Have you had her hearing tested?"

"I never saw the need. Hope is four years old, and she has never spoken a word. What other explanation could there be?" Mrs. Wainwright waved a bejeweled hand in a dismissive gesture. "My widowed sister died giving birth to Hope. I have done my Christian duty by the child, Miss Casey. My husband and I have given Hope a home. We have put food in her mouth and clothes on her back."

Mariah took note of the scuffed shoes and coarse, shapeless garment Hope wore. "What do you wish to speak to me about, Mrs. Wainwright?"

"I want to send Hope to school with Callista. She appears to be of normal intelligence. Of course I realize she will never be able to learn much, but I thought perhaps you could teach her something."

Mariah knew she should refuse—Hope was much too young to begin school—but the little girl's sad eyes tore at her heart.

"Mr. Butler is president of the school board. It would be necessary to seek his permission before allowing a child of such tender years to attend school."

"Of course. Come, Hope." Felicia Wainwright clutched the little girl's hand and set course in Sherman Butler's direction. Mariah followed in her wake.

❧

Sherman saw Felicia Wainwright bearing down on them, followed by Miss Casey.

"Mrs. Wainwright is heading our way," Karl Braun said. "Wonder what she wants."

"I guess we'll soon find out," Tom Brady said.

"Guess so," Sherman agreed. "I only hope Miss Casey doesn't resign and head back to Ohio before the school year even begins."

The woman's breathless arrival precluded further conversation. Mrs. Wainwright fanned her perspiring face with a chunky hand. "Gentlemen, I'm glad you are all here. Miss Casey wants to speak to you."

"Is there a problem, Miss Casey?" Sherman asked.

"Mrs. Wainwright wishes to enroll her niece in school. I told her she would need your permission. Hope is only four years old."

"I delivered this little girl," Dr. Brady said. "As I recall it was late July. When is Hope's birthday, Mrs. Wainwright?"

The woman's face reddened. "July twenty-ninth."

"So she is barely four years old." Karl Braun shook his head. "Miss Casey will have her hands full as it is. A four-year-old child has no place in school."

"What is your recommendation, Miss Casey?" Sherman Butler asked.

Mariah looked down into the sad, blue eyes of the small girl. "I think Hope should come to school tomorrow."

"What do you think, gentlemen?" Sherman asked.

"Maybe we should discuss this in private," Karl Braun said.

The three excused themselves and moved a few feet away from the women. Mariah leaned down. "Would you like to come to school, Hope?"

"There's no use asking her what she wants, Miss Casey." The Wainwright woman's thinly arched brows drew together in a scowl. "I told you she's dumb as a post."

When the little girl looked up at her aunt, Mariah saw a dewdrop of moisture clinging to her long, black lashes.

"Everything will be all right, Hope," she whispered in the child's perfect pink shell of an ear, hoping the girl could hear her after all.

After a few moments of earnest discussion the three men rejoined the women.

"Mrs. Wainwright, since Miss Casey is in favor of your niece attending school, Hope may start classes tomorrow with the other children." Sherman Butler's gaze shifted to Mariah. "This will be strictly on a trial basis, Miss Casey. We'll meet in one month and see how things are working out."

Mariah nodded. "Thank you, Mr. Butler. I am quite sure Hope will do fine."

"I hope so." Sherman glanced at Felicia Wainwright. "I sincerely hope so."

☙

That evening in the large kitchen at the Circle C, Sherman Butler and his two partners enjoyed a cup of coffee.

"What'd you think of the new teacher, Sherm?"

Sherman remembered the gentleness in Miss Casey's eyes when she looked at Hope. He set his cup down. "I think she will be a fine teacher, Cyrus."

"Sad though," Mac said. "She's a woman bearin' a load of pain."

"She's a might bashful, I'd reckon," Cyrus said. "But I wouldn't say she's sad."

"She's sad." Mac hobbled over to the black range. "Anyone else want a cup of coffee?" When both men declined, he returned to his chair at the long oak table. "Miss Casey's heart has been plumb broke in two."

"You read too many of them romance novels, you old coot."

"Ain't got nothin' to do with my readin' material." Mac scowled at Cyrus. "A blind man could see that lady's hurtin'."

"You sayin' I'm blind?"

"I ain't sayin' nothin' of the sort." Mac took a sip from his cup. "But iffen the boot fits, wear it."

"I'm going to bed." Sherman pushed back his chair and left the two old friends wrangling over the new schoolteacher's heart, whether it was shattered or just nonexistent.

six

Mariah stood facing her students. At least forty pairs of eyes looked back at her. Her pupils ranged in age from the diminutive Hope to a hulking young man who could barely squeeze into a desk. She had heard some of the older male teachers in Ohio talk about their experiences in backwoods schools. Sometimes older boys came to make trouble. A tremor of fear coursed through her.

Her father's Bible lay on the desk in front of her. She ran her fingers over the worn leather cover. "We will stand for the opening prayer," she said. "Then you may be seated during a short reading from the scriptures."

The children obediently rose to their feet.

Mariah tried to discern her new students' thoughts as she read the familiar passage. " 'Weeping may endure for a night, but joy cometh in the morning.' " Mariah closed the Bible. "That concludes the first five verses of the Thirtieth Psalm. I will read a short passage to you each morning except Friday. I want each of you to memorize a Bible verse during the week and be prepared to recite each Friday after opening exercises. Yes, Callista?"

The blond second grader lowered her hand and stood beside her desk. "Can we say 'Jesus wept'?"

"I would prefer you put a bit more thought into it. Begin memorizing tonight."

"Miss Butler wouldn't let us say 'Jesus wept.' " Callista twirled a blond ringlet around her finger. "What about Hope? She can't memorize. Is she going to get a whipping because she—"

"Take your seat, Callista." Mariah glanced at the wide-eyed little girl sitting at the first grade table. Her scuffed, too-big shoes didn't even reach the floor. "No one is going to be whipped."

She picked up the attendance book. "When I call your name please respond by raising your hand."

❧

Although it had seemed an insurmountable task, by the end of the week Mariah knew each student by name. As Karl Braun had assured her, although occasionally mischievous, they were well-behaved, obedient children.

Despite her efforts to remain aloof, the tiny girl at the first grade table tugged at her heartstrings. She found comfort in Hope and L. K. Braun's friendship. The sturdy six-year-old was very protective of Hope. Though the little girl didn't speak, Mariah noticed the two children always played together at recess.

Every spare moment, Mariah and Gladys worked on Mariah's house. They painted the dark woodwork sparkling white and covered the walls with colorful new wallpaper. Mariah hung blinds at the tall windows and topped them with white lace curtains. When they were finished, they stood back and admired their handiwork. Even vacant the house looked bright and cheerful.

"I like it," Gladys said.

"Mother would say it was garish," Mariah replied. "But I've lived in darkness for the last time, Cousin Gladys. I bought a new parlor suite after the auction of my parents' estate. Wait until you see it."

Mariah especially liked her bedroom paper with the full-blown red roses, and the small adjoining room she had designated as a sewing room and papered in a yellow floral. She papered the living room and dining room in blue stripes. The kitchen was done in green ivy.

In mid-September Mariah's belongings arrived, and she settled into her new house.

The following Sunday Joanna and Tom Brady invited her to dinner. Though she longed to become better acquainted with Joanna, she hesitated. If not for her cousin Gladys's insistence that she go, she would never have found the courage to accept the invitation.

A simple sign in front of the two-story house announced T. BRADY, M.D. A wide front porch, furnished with comfortable wicker chairs and a swing, spanned the front of the house.

Dr. Brady let the two women out, then turned the buggy toward the barn on the other side of the road.

Mariah followed Joanna across the porch and into a large foyer. "This is our waiting room," Joanna said. "Daddy's office and the surgery are on the right side of the hall. The parlor and dining room are on the left, and the kitchen is at the end of this hall." She gestured toward the staircase. "Our bedrooms are upstairs. You can leave your hat and gloves on the hall table if you would like."

After hanging her hat on a hook, Mariah folded her gloves and laid them on the table along with her purse. "Your home is very inviting."

"Thank you." Joanna smiled as she removed her own hat and gloves. "Since Mama passed, it sometimes seems empty."

Mariah followed Joanna down the hall to the cozy kitchen. "What can I do to help?"

"Everything is done unless you would like to slice bread while I make gravy. Then we'll get everything on the table. Daddy and I usually take our meals in the kitchen, but I thought since today is a special occasion we would eat in the dining room."

Carrying the platter of bread, she followed Joanna into the dining room. An empty invalid's chair sat in the corner. "It was Mama's," Joanna said. "She was an invalid for several years before God called her home. It was my privilege to care for her."

At first she thought the girl's remark facetious, but the tenderness of Joanna's expression when she looked at the chair dispelled that notion.

They placed the last bowls on the table as Tom Brady appeared in the doorway. "You may enter, sir," his daughter announced with a smile. "Dinner is served."

Joanna was a wonderful cook. Although the father and daughter's lighthearted banter was foreign to her, Mariah enjoyed the meal.

As they lingered over coffee and dessert, Dr. Brady asked her a few questions about her teaching experience in Ohio. Mariah gave each question careful consideration before answering.

"I realize it is different than what you were accustomed to, but do you enjoy teaching in a country school, Miss Casey?"

"It is very different," she agreed. "I taught second graders for many years. I'm not accustomed to older children." She laid down her fork. "I have one student—a young man named Mark Hopkins—who is twenty-one years old."

"I'm so happy that Mark is in school," Joanna said. "He's a couple of years older than I, but we started together. He was only there a few days before his father took him out to work."

"An eight-year-old child!" Mariah exclaimed.

"It isn't that unusual, Miss Casey." Dr. Brady leaned forward. "Ben Hopkins needed help proving up his land. Mark was his oldest child and only son."

"Mr. Hopkins should have realized the boy needed to be in school."

"Ben Hopkins is a good man. He only did what he felt was necessary."

"Mark is a sweet, gentle, hardworking young man," Joanna said. "Everyone loves him."

"Ben and Nora Hopkins have done an exemplary job of raising Mark and his sisters. They are all dedicated Christians." The doctor pushed aside his empty plate to rest his elbows on the table. Steepling his fingers under his chin, he said, "Not many families can make that claim."

"The Brauns appear to be another such family," Mariah remarked. "L. K. Braun is only six years old, but he has taken it upon himself to be Hope's protector. The two of them are inseparable."

"Karl and Hilda Braun are raising their children to be compassionate, caring people," Tom Brady said. "I dare say they are well-behaved and respectful, as well."

At Mariah's nod of affirmation, the doctor smiled. "Karl Braun accepts nothing less from his children. Mr. Braun is strict, but he's also fair. Along with discipline, the Braun children receive a boundless supply of love."

"The Brauns' eldest daughter is a friend of my cousin Lucille," Mariah said.

"Gretchen Braun, Lucille, and Carrie Butler have always been—as you remarked about L. K. and little Hope— inseparable," said Dr. Brady.

"Carrie and Gretchen were in my grade at school," Joanna said. "Six of us graduated the same year."

"There are only two in this year's graduating class," Mariah said. "Henry Carson and Jay Braun."

"We had Gretchen Braun, Carrie Butler, Becky Colton, Jake Phillips, Clay Shepherd, and me. Three of us stayed in Cedar Bend, and three of us left. Becky is living with her aunt in Missouri. Jake went away to college." Joanna sighed. "I don't know where Clay is."

"Clay Shepherd's mother died when he was little more than a baby," Dr. Brady explained. "His father was a drifter. The year they spent in Cedar Bend was probably the longest Shepherd tarried anywhere. Clay spent a lot of time here."

He glanced at the invalid's chair in the corner, and his face gentled. "My wife loved the boy, and I believe he was fond of her."

"It has been five years since I last saw Clay," Joanna added. "I still pray for him every day."

Joanna began to clear the table. Mariah rose to help her. As they worked in companionable silence, Mariah hoped that Joanna was actually enjoying being with her as much as she was enjoying the company of this tenderhearted young woman. A spark of belief that she had found someone to care about and who would care about her flickered in her heart.

❧

Mariah had just concluded opening exercises the following morning when the door opened. Every head swiveled as the visitor stepped into the classroom. Mariah rose from her chair, her heart beating a staccato. "Mr. Butler, please come in."

"I thought I would drop in and observe your class for a few minutes," the auburn-haired rancher said with a warm smile.

"Of course. Please have a seat."

He walked to the front of the room and sat down in the chair in the corner. "Go on as usual, Miss Casey. Just forget I'm here."

Mariah took a deep breath. "All right, children. Get out your history books." As Mariah moved about the classroom, she tried to keep her mind off the man sitting in the corner. Her teaching had been observed before. She knew what was expected of her. With an effort, Mariah turned her attention to her students.

❧

Sherman watched as Mariah stopped at each row of desks. As soon as she had the older ones settled, she moved to the table of first graders. Mark Hopkins came to the front of the room to join them. Sherman admired the young man. It must take a tremendous amount of courage to sit around a table with such small classmates, sounding out the words Miss Casey printed on the blackboard.

Sherman enjoyed the sound of the teacher's voice. It was soft and feminine but clear and easily understood. As she stood at the blackboard, a wisp of hair escaped her severe bun and curled against the back of her neck. He wondered why such an appealing woman wore her hair in such an unbecoming style. It was almost as though she were trying to make herself unattractive.

A short time later, he left the small school, thankful he had finally listened to Mrs. Jacobs and hired Mariah Casey. From what he had observed, she was more than competent as an educator. He was surprised to find himself also wondering what was hidden inside this teacher's heart.

※

That afternoon Mariah had her second visitor. Her last student had straggled out, and she was putting her desk in order when Felicia Wainwright barged through the door. "Miss Casey, how dare you punish my darling Callista!"

Mariah folded her hands on top of her desk. "Please have a seat, Mrs. Wainwright."

"I will not." The woman rested her hands on the desk and leaned forward until her face was inches from Mariah's. "Callista told me what you did to her. I will not allow it. Do you understand me, madam? I will not allow my precious baby to be humiliated."

The woman's face was red, and a blood vessel throbbed in her temple. Mariah rose and moved the chair from the corner. "Please sit down, Mrs. Wainwright."

The woman dropped into the chair placed beside the desk while Mariah went to the water bucket beside the back door and poured a cup of water. She thrust the cup into the woman's hand before returning to her chair behind the desk. "Why don't you tell me what this is about?"

The woman set the cup on the corner of the desk and fanned herself with a dainty linen handkerchief until she got her breath. "My baby told me she was forced to stand in the corner for fifteen minutes today."

"Did Callista tell you why she was punished?"

"She said that you don't like her."

Callista was not a likable child. No one in the classroom liked her. "I do not punish children because I do not like them. It is my responsibility to uphold integrity in the classroom. Callista copied off Jenny Carson's paper."

"I don't believe it." Felicia puffed up like a toad. "My child would never cheat. You're taking the side of the Carson girl because her father is the pastor at your church."

"Mrs. Wainwright, the truth is not always easy to hear." Mariah laced her fingers together on the desktop and took a deep breath. "Callista is still young enough to be malleable, but I fear if you do not take her in hand soon it may be—"

The woman's voice rose. "What do you mean 'take her in hand'?"

"Callista cheats, Mrs. Wainwright."

The woman began to sputter.

Mariah held up a hand. "Please hear me out. Your daughter lies. She torments Hope. She—"

"Hope!" The word burst from the woman. "This is all about Hope, isn't it? Callista told me you favored that little foundling over her."

"Callista's behavior has nothing to do with her cousin." An image of the tiny girl's huge, blue eyes passed through Mariah's mind. "Hope is an innocent child."

"You don't like the way I am raising the child."

"I didn't say that. I only—"

"You can have Hope." Her voice dropped. "Take her, Miss Casey."

People didn't give children away. Did they? Mariah leaned

forward. "What are you saying?"

"I don't want her." Two fat tears rolled down the woman's face. "Every time I look at her, I see Carly."

"Your sister?"

"Mama and Papa never loved me after she came. Everyone always preferred Carly. They thought she was perfect. By the time she was fifteen, there were young men hanging around her like bees around a honeysuckle vine. I never had a suitor until Harry. When he asked me to marry him, I jumped at the chance. We moved to Cedar Bend, and five years after our wedding, God gave me Callista. Carly married when she was nineteen. After Mama and Papa passed away, Carly and her husband, Ned, came for a visit. They had been married less than a year, but already Carly was expecting. Everything always came so easy for her. Ned was killed in a riding accident—his horse threw him and his neck was broken. Two months later Hope was born and Carly died."

Mrs. Wainwright sat weeping into her handkerchief. Mariah quietly waited for the woman to regain control of herself. She didn't like Felicia Wainwright, but she knew what it was to be unloved. The woman drew a shuddering breath. She looked at Mariah through swollen, red-rimmed eyes. "The last words Carly spoke were to tell me she loved me and to ask me to take care of her baby." She twisted the damp handkerchief. "Every time I look at Hope and Callista, I see Carly and myself. I want to love Hope, but I can't. Please take her, Miss Casey."

Mariah looked down at her interlaced fingers. Hope was a child, a precious gift from God. She thought of the little girl's sorrow-filled eyes. A deep longing coursed through her. A yearning she could not deny.

"Harry has a job offer in California. We plan on leaving at the end of the week. You will never see us again, Miss Casey. Hope will forget us."

"Yes." Mariah's clenched hands trembled. "Yes, I will take Hope."

"You will?" Felicia Wainwright stood. "I. . . Oh, thank you! Thank you, Miss Casey. Harry will bring Hope and her things to your house this evening. I'll just collect Callista's books now. I think it would be best if she didn't return to school."

Mariah remained seated for several minutes after Felicia Wainwright left. Her father's closed Bible lay on the desk in front of her. *What have I done, Lord?* She ran her fingers over the worn leather cover. *I know nothing of raising a child. Please give me wisdom, Father.*

&

The parlor clock chimed seven times. Mariah moved the lace curtain aside to peer into the empty street. Felicia Wainwright had said her husband would bring Hope in the evening. Had she changed her mind? Mariah resumed pacing. In the room next to her own, the narrow brass bed was freshly made up and ready. She stood looking down at the four-patch quilt, then sank into the small rocking chair beside the bed. Hope wasn't coming. Felicia Wainwright was an overwrought, impulsive woman. She would never give up her niece.

A sharp knock at the front door brought Mariah to her feet. The slight man standing on the porch held his hat and a carpetbag in one hand. The other hand rested on the small girl's shoulder. "Miss Casey, I've brought Hope."

Mariah looked down into the little girl's wide, blue eyes. "Welcome home, Hope."

seven

Mariah felt a moment of panic after the door closed behind Harry Wainwright. Standing in the middle of the parlor floor with the carpetbag beside her, Hope looked as lost and confused as Mariah felt.

"Well, Hope, I am pleased to have you here." Mariah spoke to Hope, believing the girl could probably hear, but she also made gestures along with her words just in case Felicia Wainwright was correct about the girl being deaf. "Let's get you settled in." She picked up the little girl's bag. As small as the bag was, it was only half full. Hope followed her to the bedroom. "This will be your room. The bed was mine when I was a small girl. I didn't have time to decorate it for you, but we will do that later. I thought you might want to choose things for it yourself. Do you think you might like that?"

Hope watched while Mariah put away her few possessions. At the bottom of the bag was a package wrapped in brown butcher paper.

"What is this?" Mariah sat down in the rocking chair. Hope watched as she unwrapped a photograph of a young couple. The man was fair-haired and handsome. The girl had dark hair and large eyes that appeared luminous even in the sepia-toned photograph. "This must be your mother and father, Hope. See how beautiful she is. You look exactly like her."

An envelope with her name on it fell to the floor. Mariah picked it up and slipped it into her pocket. "I baked cookies for you this afternoon. Do you like oatmeal and raisin? How would you like to have cookies and milk for a bedtime snack?"

Mariah held out the plate of cookies, and the little girl smiled brightly.

Sitting at the kitchen table, Mariah watched Hope eat a cookie. *Poor child! Mrs. Wainwright didn't tell her anything. She has no idea why she is here or what is happening. Father, please help me to make her understand.*

"Hope, I need to explain some things to you." The child gave no indication she heard. Mariah covered a small hand with her own. "You are going to live here with me, Hope."

The little girl looked up, her blue eyes questioning. "Forever," Mariah said.

Hope pulled her hand from under Mariah's. She took one of the two cookies that remained on the saucer and thrust it into Mariah's hand. It was on the tip of the woman's tongue to say she never ate cookies. She bit back the words and poured herself a glass of milk.

After the snack, Mariah helped Hope get ready for bed. When Hope was in her nightgown, Mariah unbraided the little girl's hair. "You have beautiful hair," she said as she pulled the brush through the thick silken tresses. She braided her hair—loosely this time—and tucked her into bed. She read aloud from a Bible storybook that she had owned since she was a child until Hope's eyes closed in sleep.

For a time she sat in the rocking chair, looking at the little girl. The enormity of what lay ahead overwhelmed her. She put the book on the table at her side. Kneeling beside the small bed, she prayed for Hope to be healthy and happy. She prayed for her to grow up secure in the knowledge that she was loved and wanted. Most importantly, she prayed that she would come to know and love the Lord.

She forgot the letter in her pocket until she was preparing for bed. Sitting on the edge of her bed, she read Felicia Wainwright's letter. It was mostly a self-serving plea for understanding. She said she didn't want Mariah to think badly of her as she had done her best to give her sister's child a good home. "It was unfair," she wrote, "that Carly always had so much, while I had so little." At first, Mariah felt no pity for the selfish woman. But as anger began to form, a still, small voice reminded her that she wasn't as different from Felicia Wainwright as she wanted to believe. Pain from her own mother's sharp words still remained deep in her heart and caused her to say and do things she always regretted later. She dropped to her knees and prayed for Felicia Wainwright to find peace of heart and mind. She also found herself praying God would grant her the same.

❧

Getting a four-year-old up, fed, dressed, and ready for the day was more time-consuming than Mariah could ever have imagined. By the time they arrived at school, more than half her students were standing on the porch waiting for her. Twelve-year-old Mabel Carson came to meet her. "Miss Casey, we were afraid you had fallen ill. Are you all right?"

"I'm fine, Mabel, but I appreciate your concern." Mariah unlocked the door and led the children inside.

After prayer and scripture reading, Mariah called the roll. When all eyes turned to Callista's empty desk, Mariah told the class that the Wainwright family was moving to California and Callista wouldn't be back. No one asked why Hope was still present in the classroom, or why she had arrived that morning with the teacher.

Mariah noticed Hope hesitate beside Callista's empty desk as the children filed out to recess that morning. L. K. whispered something to her—he obviously thought she could hear, too—then took her hand, and the two children walked out the door together. When they came back inside, Hope passed her cousin's empty place without a second glance. Mariah saw no sign of the Wainwright family the rest of the week. Still, she was uneasy until she knew they had left town.

On Friday she dismissed school early and took Hope to

Dr. Brady's office. After a thorough examination the doctor handed the little girl a peppermint stick and sent her from the room with Joanna.

"Miss Casey, have a seat." Mariah perched on the edge of a straight chair across the desk from the doctor. "I can find nothing wrong with Hope. There is no malformation of the ear. She reacts to sound."

"I knew it. I knew she could hear."

"As far as I can tell, she can also speak. It is my opinion that when she feels secure, she will speak." He adjusted a cup on his desk. "I understand the Wainwrights left this morning."

"Yes." Mariah breathed a sigh of relief. "I was afraid she would want Hope back."

"I never thought she would give the child up." The doctor's smile lit up his rugged face. "The Lord must have moved her heart."

Mariah thought of the letter Hope's aunt had left her. "He did indeed," she agreed. She then added to herself, *Her heart is not the only one God is moving. Thank You, Lord!*

&

Hope skipped along at Mariah's side as they walked to the mercantile.

Mariah had been to the store several times, but Mr. Harris had always been the only one in attendance. She cast around in her mind trying to recall where she had seen the cheerful woman who greeted her today.

"You don't remember me, do you? Now don't you be embarrassed, Miss Casey. You have had to get used to so many new faces. I'm Ettie Harris. I've seen you at church, but I don't believe we've ever been formally introduced."

"Of course," Mariah said. "You are the pianist."

"I'm also the pastor's mother-in-law, and I teach Sunday school, as well. From what I have heard, you are doing a wonderful job with all our children." The middle-aged woman beamed. "The Carson children are my grandchildren."

"Pastor Carson's children are a delight." Mariah smiled. "I don't know what I would do without Mabel."

"Yes, Mabel told me you chose her to help the little ones learn their letters. She tells me she wants to be a teacher just like you." After a brief exchange of pleasantries, Mrs. Harris got down to business. "What can I help you with, Miss Casey?"

"I need to buy some things for Hope." Mariah took a folded piece of paper from her pocket. "I have a list, but there may be other items that I have forgotten."

The woman took the slip of paper from Mariah. "My, this is quite a list."

"I want to replace everything she brought with her."

Mrs. Harris slipped Mariah's list into her pocket. "Fred is in the storeroom. I'll get him in here to wait on folks while I help you."

After Mrs. Harris turned the few customers in the store over to her husband, the two women selected underwear and stockings for Hope and piled them neatly on the front counter.

"Now," Mariah said, "we need to look at shoes."

"Certainly." Mrs. Harris led the way to a corner of the store. "You sit right here in this chair, Hope."

While Hope was being seated, Mrs. Harris went through a door leading to the back of the store and returned with two boxes. "These are the finest shoes made for children," she said, sitting down on a small stool in front of Hope. "Let's pull your shoes off, honey, and try these." Hope extended her feet. Mrs. Harris pulled off the old shoes and slipped on the new ones. "That appears to be a perfect fit. Let me get the button hook and you can walk around in them."

Mariah noticed that Hope was responding to all that Mrs. Harris asked, and a warm feeling enveloped her heart. *Maybe she is beginning to feel secure—and loved.*

While Hope walked back and forth on the scrap of carpet, Mrs. Harris chatted with Mariah. "The shoes your little one is wearing are seventy-five cents a pair. I have a pair of higher quality that sells for a dollar sixty, but as fast as they grow at that age I would go with the less expensive pair."

"I am submitting myself to your expertise, Mrs. Harris. Though I have been with children most of my life, I must confess that I know very little of the practical aspects of raising them."

"Don't you fret, Miss Casey. You just follow your instincts and you'll do fine." She patted Mariah's hand. "I raised six children. If you have any questions don't hesitate to ask me or one of the other women at church. We will help in any way we can."

"Thank you, Mrs. Harris." Mariah's eyes were on Hope as she skipped across the rug. "I appreciate your thoughtfulness."

Hope climbed into the chair beside Mariah.

"Did you find the shoes comfortable, dear?" Mrs. Harris reached a hand toward Hope's feet. The little girl put her feet as far underneath the chair as possible. "Well," the woman said, laughing, "I believe she likes them."

A smile tugged at the corners of Mariah's mouth. "It would seem you have made a sale, Mrs. Harris. Is it all right if she keeps the shoes on?"

"Of course it is." The woman patted Hope's dark head. "You be sure and wear those pretty shoes to my Sunday school class. Your mama says you can keep them, honey."

At the word *mama* Hope looked up at Mariah. *Mama!* After one stunned moment, a feeling of joy washed over Mariah. "Let's look at some dress goods," she said.

"We have a wonderful dressmaker just a few doors down the street. You'll remember Eunice Wright from church," Mrs. Harris said.

"Yes, of course, but I brought my sewing machine with me from Ohio." Mariah stood. "I want to make Hope's clothes myself."

Mrs. Harris smiled understandingly and led them to a table piled high with fabric. Mariah and the shopkeeper selected a length of pale gray calico strewn with blue flowers, a blue plaid gingham, and a dark blue piece with multicolored flowers. A rack of ready-made dresses caught Mariah's eye. She looked through them and took one that appeared to be Hope's size from the rack.

"That one is seventy-five cents," Mrs. Harris said.

The dress was expensive—more than the fabric for the other three together—but she didn't have time to make Hope a dress before church Sunday morning. "Is there somewhere she could try it on?"

"Of course there is." She took the dress from Mariah. "Come with me, Hope. Your mama wants you to try this on." She took Hope's small hand. "We'll come back and surprise Mama."

Mama. Would she ever become accustomed to that word in relation to herself? *Thank You, Lord. Thank You. Thank You. Help me to be a good mama to this precious little girl You have entrusted to my care.*

"Well, now what do you think of us?" Mrs. Harris stood before her with Hope. The dress fit as if it had been made for the little girl.

"It's perfect in every way," Mariah replied.

Hope twirled around, causing the full skirt to flare out. Mrs. Harris chuckled. Mariah, no longer able to hold back, let her own laughter overflow.

&

"You get ever'thing loaded, Sherm?" The storekeeper leaned against the counter.

"I think that'll do me for this trip," Sherman Butler answered absently, his attention on the two women and the little girl at the back of the store.

The storekeeper followed his gaze. "Did you hear that Mrs. Wainwright gave that little girl to Miss Casey?"

"No, I hadn't heard," Sherman said.

"Yep. The Wainwrights moved to California. Left first light this morning." The storekeeper leaned in closer. "Gave that little girl away like an unwanted puppy."

"Miss Casey took her?"

"Yep. They been in here the better part of an hour. The schoolteacher's buying the store out." He rested his hand on a pile of clothing. "This here is all for that little girl."

The women and the child moved slowly to the front of the store. Miss Casey's cheeks were pink, and her eyes sparkled. Sherman had always thought she was attractive, but today he realized how pretty she really was. He tipped his hat. "Mrs. Harris. Miss Casey. Who is this little princess?" He smiled down at Hope. "That is a very pretty dress you have on, sweetheart."

"She refuses to take her new dress off." Mariah laughed. "I am afraid she will insist on sleeping in it."

He found Miss Casey's laugh delightful. "I know what to do about that." He lifted Hope up and sat her on the counter. "Mr. Harris has some gumdrops here. Would you like some?"

Hope looked from the jar of brightly colored candies to Miss Casey then up at the tall man. "Give this young lady a penny's worth of gumdrops, Fred."

The storekeeper handed the small bag to Hope. "You mustn't eat any of these until after you get home and change your dress," Sherman said. "All right?"

Hope's lower lip stuck out the slightest bit, but she nodded. He couldn't resist hugging the little girl before he stood her back on the floor.

"Thank you, Mr. Butler, but it wasn't necessary that you buy her candy."

"It was my pleasure, Miss Casey." Sherman smiled. "Just don't let her have a candy until she takes off her new dress."

"No, I won't."

Sherman watched as Mariah counted out the money for her purchases. "You are never going to be able to carry all this home," Mrs. Harris said. "If you like, Fred can deliver it all after we close the store."

"Yes, I would appreciate that."

"If you don't mind riding in a buckboard, I'd be happy to see you and Hope home with your packages," Sherman offered.

The color rose in Mariah's face as she looked up at the smiling man. "Thank you, but I wouldn't wish to be an imposition."

"You wouldn't be. It's on my way." He picked up two of the bags. "I'll load this for you."

Mariah offered no further protest as she and Hope followed Sherman outside. He stowed her purchases in the buckboard, then lifted Hope into the middle of the wide bench seat before taking Mariah's elbow and assisting her onto the seat beside Hope.

"Miss Casey, are you getting settled in?" he asked as soon as they were on their way.

"Yes. I believe I am." Mariah glanced down at the small girl beside her. "My life has certainly changed in the last few weeks."

Sherman chuckled. "I should imagine it has."

After that, though Mariah responded briefly to his comments, Sherman's attempts at small talk seemed to fall on unreceptive ears, and the remainder of the short trip was completed in silence.

Soon they drew up in front of the neat, clapboard cottage. Sherman jumped from the buckboard and lifted Hope to the ground. When he extended a helping hand to Mariah, she hesitated for the briefest moment before placing her hand in his and climbing down from the buckboard.

Sherman continued to hold her slender, gloved hand even after she was standing in the street facing him.

"It was most kind of you to see us home, Mr. Butler." She blushed and gently extracted her hand from his.

"I'm glad I was there and could be of assistance." Sherman hurried to the back of the buckboard and carried Mariah's purchases up the steps of the front porch.

"If you leave the packages beside the door I will take them inside."

"I'll be happy to carry them in for you."

"No, please." Mariah glanced at the neighboring houses, and again pink tinted the delicate ivory of her face. "I can carry them in."

"As you wish." Sherman deposited the parcels beside the door and tipped his hat to the lady. "Good day, Miss Casey." He rested a hand on Hope's head. "Remember, little Miss Hope, no gumdrops until you have changed your dress."

Sherman whistled as he drove out of town.

eight

The Bradys were having dinner at Mariah's. There were so many last-minute details to attend to Sunday morning that Mariah and Hope were late for Sunday school. Though it was only a couple of minutes, for Mariah, who was unaccustomed to being late, it seemed like hours. After seeing Hope settled in her class, she slid into the pew beside Joanna Brady. The young woman smiled at her, and Mariah smiled back.

"Second Timothy, chapter 1," Joanna whispered.

Mariah quickly found her place and settled back to catch her breath. Hope hadn't looked too happy when she left her with Mrs. Harris, but Mariah refused to worry. The little girl was in good hands. She would be fine.

Pastor Carson was the teacher of the Sunday school class. *A very good teacher,* Mariah thought. After the reading of each passage, he encouraged discussion. It fell to Mariah to read the fifth verse. " 'When I call to remembrance the unfeigned faith that is in thee, which dwelt first in thy grandmother Lois, and thy mother Eunice; and I am persuaded that in thee also.' "

"Every morning and evening my father read to us from the Bible," the pastor said, "but it was my mother who knelt beside our beds with us and taught us to pray. How many of you remember your mothers praying with you?"

Almost every hand raised. "Mama died when I was small," Carrie Nolan said, "but I remember her praying. When she knew she would be leaving me while I was still very young, she left a series of letters for me to read when I was older. Those letters, and her Bible with her favorite passages marked and the notes in the margins, mean the world to me."

"My mother always sang hymns while she prepared breakfast," Carrie's husband, Lucas, volunteered. "That is one of my fondest memories of her. Those early memories of Ma singing 'Amazing Grace' had a great deal to do with my own salvation."

"As you all know, Mama was unwell for many years," Joanna said. "The last few years she was an invalid, it was my privilege to care for her. We spent many hours together studying the Word, singing, and praying. That time with my mother is a priceless gift that I will always cherish."

Mariah listened quietly while several others in the class spoke of their early training times with godly mothers.

"Miss Casey," the pastor spoke, "do you have anything to add? I know your father was a pastor, but your mother surely had a tremendous influence on your life, as well."

Mariah looked down at the Bible lying open on her lap. Mother had surely influenced her life, but not in a way she could share with her Sunday school class. She looked into the pastor's caring gray eyes and said the only thing she could say. "My mother was a very beautiful woman. When I was small I idolized her."

When she said no more, the pastor went on to the next verse.

❧

Mariah was walking out of church with the Bradys when a horse galloped up and a distraught-looking man flung himself from the saddle and rushed up to them. "Doc Brady, Lizzie's took sick. She needs you."

"Of course, Sid. You go on home. We'll be right behind you." He turned to Mariah. "I'm sorry about dinner, Miss Casey."

"It's all right," Mariah said. "We will do it another time."

"I'm sorry, Mariah," Joanna added to her father's apology. "Lizzie's labor is always difficult. We will probably be out there until sometime in the night."

Trying to hide her disappointment, Mariah assured them they would simply reschedule. She and Hope watched the Bradys' carriage turn on to the street.

"Well, Hope, it looks as though we'll have dinner alone."

"Not necessarily," a deep voice behind her said. Mariah turned and looked up into Sherman Butler's blue eyes. "Why don't you come out to the Circle C? Mac cooks enough for an army."

"I'd reckon we'd be happy to have you an' the little 'un." An elderly man Mariah assumed was Mac stepped from behind Sherman. "You an' the little lady kin ride out with me in the buggy."

Mariah was on the verge of refusing when she looked down at Hope. The little girl was looking up at her, blue eyes alight with anticipation.

"We accept your invitation." Mariah thought of the two pies at home. "Under one condition. That I be allowed to stop at my house and pick up dessert."

"I think that can be arranged." A wide grin revealed the strong, white teeth framed by Mr. Butler's full, auburn mustache. He escorted Mariah and Hope to the buggy, then mounted his horse and rode away with several other men.

"Lucas and Carrie will be long directly," Mac said, as he guided the horse out of the churchyard, "but we ain't waitin' fer 'em."

"Mr. and Mrs. Nolan will be there?"

"Yep! They'll be wherever there's a decent meal." The little man grinned. "I tried my best to teach Carrie to cook afore she wuz married, but she jist never seemed to have a knack fer it."

"I heard her tell Cousin Gladys she couldn't cook, but I thought she was being modest," Mariah said. "I imagined she could do anything."

"Carrie ain't never been known fer bein' modest 'bout her accomplishments." The old man chuckled. "And ain't nobody kin do ever'thing, Miz Casey."

"No, I suppose not," Mariah agreed, feeling somewhat better about spending an afternoon with Carrie Nolan. By the time Mac pulled the buggy to a stop in front of Mariah's house, Hope had become a soft weight against her. Mac put his arm around the sleeping child and cradled her head against his side. "You run on and git what you need," he said. "Me an' the little lady will be jist fine."

Mariah only hesitated a moment before climbing down from the buggy and hurrying inside.

۲

"Sherm tells me you keered fer yer ma back in Ohio," Mac said, as soon as they resumed their journey.

"Yes, ever since I was eighteen." Mariah arranged the sleeping child so that she lay on the seat with her head cradled in her lap. "My parents were in a buggy accident. Father was killed. Mother's leg was broken, and her face was scarred."

"Missus Jacobs told Sherman that yer ma was left an invalid."

"The leg was badly broken and didn't heal properly. After the accident Mother walked with a pronounced limp. Then, of course, there were the scars."

The little man frowned. "I figgered it wuz worse than that."

"I'm sure Mother inferred that in her letters to Cousin Gladys, and for her it was devastating. My mother was a very beautiful woman, Mr. McDougal. Her life ended with the accident. It would have been more merciful for her if she had died with Father."

Mariah could hardly believe she was having such a personal conversation with a stranger. But there was something about Mac McDougal that inspired confidence. Still, she didn't like to remember the years she had spent trying to please her mother.

A quote from Shakespeare came to mind. *What's gone and past help, should be past grief.* She could do nothing to change what had happened the first thirty-six years of her life. Mariah ran a gentle hand over the dark ringlets of Hope's silky hair. The past was best left in the past. The future lay sleeping in her lap.

"You love that little gal a lot, don't cha?" Mac's faded blue eyes rested briefly on the sleeping child.

"Having Hope is a dream come true."

"Looks to me like yer doin' a mighty fine job with 'er."

"Thank you, Mr. McDougal, but I feel so inadequate." Mariah glanced at the little man before looking back down at the child. "I have always believed we learn our life skills from our parents. Mother wasn't an affectionate woman."

Mac pulled on his ear. "Wal, you ain't necessarily like yer ma." He glanced at Mariah. "You got a lot of love in you, Miz Casey. I kin see thet when you look at thet little girl, an' I'd reckon some things jist comes natural."

"Mother was ashamed of me." Mariah felt the pain crowd up into her throat. "She often said she didn't understand how she could have given birth to such a tall, homely child."

"No offense, ma'am, but I reckon yer ma was a right foolish woman." Mac cleared his throat. "You are tall, there's no denyin' thet, but yer fur from homely, Miz Casey. Don't you never let no one tell you otherwise."

The man's kindness touched her. Mariah looked away to hide the tears that threatened to overflow.

A few minutes later they left the main road and passed under an arched sign that read CIRCLE C RANCH. Hope stirred, sat up, and looked around with sleep-dazed eyes. "This here's the Circle C, little lady. The house is up there at the end of this lane."

The ranch house was a rambling one-story structure of cedar and native stone. Mariah had never seen such a dwelling, but she immediately liked it.

As soon as the buggy drew up in front of the house, Sherman

hurried to meet them. "Welcome to the Circle C," he said as he gave Mariah a helping hand. When he reached for Hope she stood up on the buggy seat and leaped into his arms.

"Hope, don't ever do that again," Mariah scolded. "If Mr. Butler hadn't caught you, you could have fallen and been hurt."

"I wouldn't let her fall," Sherman said.

Hope looked at her, then tightened her arms around Mr. Butler's neck.

Mariah detected a mischievous gleam in the little girl's eyes. She turned away to hide her own smile. Mac was hobbling toward the house with her basket. She followed with Hope and Sherman.

"This here's my kitchen," Mac said, setting the basket on the table. "The ranch hands eat in here. Course with winter comin' on we ain't got a full crew."

Mariah looked around the large room. A huge fireplace, with a rocking chair and a small footstool in front of it, took up one wall. A long table surrounded by a dozen chairs stood in the middle of the wooden floor. A long counter, topped by shelves filled with dishes, glasses, and foodstuffs, lined one wall.

"We used to do all our cookin' in thet there fireplace," Mac said. "Thet was afore I got this here nice black range."

The black and chrome range—like everything else in the kitchen—was huge. The chrome was polished to a shine that reflected the room.

Mariah felt some comment about the range, obviously the little man's pride and joy, was in order. "It is a beautiful cookstove, Mr. McDougal," she said.

"Thet it is, Miss Casey." The little man smiled. "By the way, nobody ever calls me Mr. McDougal. I'm jist plain Mac."

Before Mariah had a chance to respond, Carrie Nolan swept through the door. "We're here," she announced. "Lucas will be in as soon as he's finished taking care of the horse. What's for dinner, Mac? I'm starving." She paused for a heartbeat when she saw Mariah. "I didn't know you were here, Miss Casey." She dismissed Mariah, and her gaze settled on the little girl clinging to Mariah's hand. "Hope, my goodness, don't you look pretty. Are you going to sit beside me at dinner?"

Hope immediately released Mariah's hand and clasped Carrie's hand. Mariah felt betrayed, though she told herself Hope was only a child. Why wouldn't she prefer the sparkling beauty of Carrie Nolan to her new mother's dull plainness? Still, no matter what she told herself, the pain in her heart was impossible to deny. The meal was delicious, but Mariah picked at her food. Mac and Sherman Butler tried to draw her into the conversation that flowed between Carrie Nolan and the four men, but she felt isolated and left out. She barely knew the people Carrie chattered on and on about. Worse yet, Hope kept looking up at the Nolan woman with wide-eyed fascination, hanging on every foolish word the young woman uttered.

At last the miserable meal was over. Mariah insisted on helping Mac clear the table, but he wouldn't allow her to do dishes. "I got me a feller thet does the cleanin' up, Mariah. You jist go in the parlor and rest."

"I have a better idea." Sherman smiled at Mariah. "How would you and Hope like to take a walk with me?"

He picked Hope up and set her on one arm. "Would you like to walk out to the corral and see the horses, Hope?"

Mr. Butler had been thoughtful to invite them to dinner. It would be impolite to refuse his offer. Besides, a walk was a perfect excuse to get away from Carrie Nolan. "A walk would be nice," Mariah said.

"Lucas and I will go with you," Carrie said, clasping her husband's arm.

"I don't reckon Sherm invited us along," Lucas drawled.

The color rose in Carrie's face. "Well, I happen to think—"

Mariah never had a chance to hear what Carrie thought.

Sherman put his free hand on her elbow and guided her out the door. He set Hope on the ground and took her tiny hand in his. Mariah took the little girl's other hand, and the three of them walked across to the corral. Sherman picked Hope up and stood her on one of the higher rails of the corral fence. She draped her arms over the top rail and clung there as though it was an everyday occurrence for her.

"She's a natural-born rancher." Sherman laughed and put his hand on the little girl's back to steady her.

Mariah already had her hand around Hope's waist. When his hand touched hers, a tingle ran all the way to her elbow. Didn't he realize that her hand was resting beneath his? What was the proper thing to do in this situation?

She should pull her hand away. She should, but the feel of that big, work-roughened hand on hers felt so good. Finally he was the one to move his hand.

"You see the pony over there, Hope?" He pointed to a black animal with white stocking feet and a matching blaze on its forehead. "Next time you come to visit I'll let you ride her. That is, if it's all right with your mama."

Hope turned sparkling blue eyes on Mariah. The pony was smaller than the other horses but still looked potentially dangerous. "I don't know," Mariah said. "Hope is rather small to ride such a large animal."

"I'll lead her around the corral," Sherman said. "She'll be perfectly safe."

"We'll see," Mariah conceded. She lifted the little girl from the fence and stood her on the ground.

"There's something in the barn Hope might like to see." Sherman pointed out the long, low bunkhouse and several other outbuildings as they strolled in the direction of the barn.

In the dim, shadowy barn, the smell of fresh hay mingled with the earthy scent of manure and warm animals. Mariah heard the faint mewling of kittens. "They're in this corner." Sherman scooped Hope up with one arm. Mariah released the little girl's hand and followed.

The man reached a hand into the straw nest and lifted out a squirming ball of yellow fur. "They don't have their eyes open yet," he said. "Would you like to hold him, Hope?"

Hope nodded, and Sherman placed the small ball of fluff in her hands. "Don't squeeze him too tight," he warned.

Hope rubbed her face against the kitten's head. "Oh!" she said; then she laughed.

Mariah had never heard the child utter a sound. That single exclamation and the joyful laugh were an affirmation of her belief that Hope would one day speak. Tears filled her eyes and she quickly turned away. Sherman stood Hope down on the straw-littered floor and put his hand on Mariah's arm. She allowed him to lead her a few steps away from the little girl.

"She has never spoken before?"

Mariah shook her head. "No," she said softly. "But I knew she could. Sometimes when children are mistreated, they try to make themselves invisible."

"Well, in that case, Hope should be talking your ear off in no time." He wiped a tear from Mariah's face with his thumb. "You're doing a wonderful job with her, Miss Casey."

Mariah's breath quickened at the touch of his hand on her face. She couldn't recall anyone ever looking at her with the tenderness she detected in his blue eyes. For a heartbeat she allowed herself to believe Sherman Butler had feelings for her. Then she stepped back from him. "Raising a child is more difficult than I could have imagined." She looked at Hope cuddling the tiny, blind kitten. "It is also the most rewarding experience of my life."

&

"Well, did you have a nice walk?" Carrie's eyes were cold, her smile false. She, her husband, Cyrus, and Mac were sitting around the big kitchen table eating Mariah's pies and drinking steaming cups of coffee.

"Yes," Mariah said. "It was quite enjoyable. Mr. Butler showed Hope the kittens."

Carrie glanced at the little girl now sitting between Mac and Cyrus. "Papa is fond of children."

"This is mighty good pie," Mac said. "The crust is so flaky it melts in yer mouth."

The other men voiced an affirmation of Mac's compliment.

"I would like to show Miss Casey the house." Carrie stood and pushed her chair under the table. "May we be excused for a few minutes?"

"Certainly, if Miss Casey has no objection." Sherman's dimples deepened. "I think the two of you should get better acquainted."

Mariah was reluctant to go with Carrie, but there seemed no valid reason not to.

"I want to show you something in the parlor." Carrie led the way into a huge room with rough stucco walls and open beams overhead. Woven wool rugs were scattered over the polished hardwood floor. The massive, leather-covered couches and chairs were deep and inviting. Bookcases filled one wall. Mariah would have loved to peruse the volumes that rested there, but Carrie led her to stand before the enormous stone fireplace.

"This is Mama, Caroline Houston Butler. I'm named for her," she said. "Wasn't she beautiful?"

Mariah looked at the portrait hanging above the fireplace. The woman was beautiful, but it was the air of contentment the artist had captured that caught Mariah's eye. Caroline Butler was a woman who knew she was valued, and it showed in her face. Her dark eyes glowed with happiness.

"She is wearing her wedding dress," Carrie said. "There is one thing you need to understand, Miss Casey." She turned to face Mariah. "Papa loved Mama with his whole heart. In the years she's been gone other women have set their caps for him, but he has never been interested. Papa and Mama are bound together for all eternity. No other woman could ever take her place in his heart. I am telling you this so you won't make a fool of yourself."

Mariah felt the hot flame of humiliation burn her face.

"We had best rejoin the others," Carrie said. "I should imagine you will want to be leaving. One of the ranch hands will drive you back to town."

When they came back into the kitchen, Mariah collected her empty pie tins with downcast eyes, too shamed to look at anyone.

"Air you all right, ma'am?" Mac asked.

The concern in the old man's voice brought a lump to Mariah's throat. "I'm fine." She fought back tears. "Tomorrow is a school day. We need to go home."

"It is getting late," Carrie said. "We should be going, too. Do you want us to have Buck hitch the buggy, Papa?"

"That would be fine," Sherman said. "Have him bring it up to the house."

"It was nice of you to come, Miss Casey." Carrie leaned down to kiss Hope. "You, too, sweetheart."

Amid a flurry of good-byes, Lucas and Carrie left.

"I got somethin' fer you." Mac set a gallon of milk on the table, along with a cheesecloth-wrapped chunk of butter and a sack of eggs.

"Oh, I couldn't—" Mariah started to protest but was cut off by Mac's insistence that she certainly could.

"You might bring us a custard pie next time you come," he said.

"Well, I don't know." Mariah blushed. "It was nice of you to have us this time, but—"

"We were hoping you would come again," Sherman said.

Mariah was saved a reply by the arrival of the buggy. "Come, Hope, we mustn't keep the gentleman waiting."

Mac gathered up the eggs, milk, and butter and put them in Mariah's basket; then they all went outside. The horses were tied to the hitching rail. Mariah looked around for the driver, but there was no sign of the ranch hand Carrie had called Buck.

"You fergit somethin', Miz Casey?" Mac asked.

"No, I just—Mrs. Nolan said a ranch hand would drive us back to town."

"That ranch hand would be me." Sherman lifted Hope into the buggy, then assisted Mariah up before climbing into the driver's seat himself.

Sherman carried the burden of the conversation on the trip to town. Every time Mariah looked at him, she heard Carrie telling her not to make a fool of herself, and her stomach twisted. She kept her gaze fixed on Hope, the rolling prairie, the glorious gold and lavender of the setting sun. Anywhere but at the man who was telling her about his partnership with Mac and Cyrus and how they built the Circle C after the war with unclaimed stock they herded to Kansas from Texas. The man who captured her thoughts and attention like no other ever had.

nine

Sherman sat in the kitchen with the two men who had been his best friends for over thirty years. "What did you think of her?"

"That Hope's a mighty cute little gal." Mac's faded blue eyes twinkled.

"I meant Miss Casey." Sherman ran his fingers through his thick, auburn hair. "Did you like her all right?"

"She seems to be a fine, God-fearin' woman," Cyrus said.

"She is." Sherman took a sip of hot coffee before setting his cup on the table.

The three men talked about other things for several minutes, then Cyrus said it was time for him to turn in and excused himself. After he went out to the bunkhouse, Mac turned a speculative eye on the younger man.

"You interested in the schoolmarm in a romantical sense?" Mac always got to the heart of the matter.

"Miss Casey is the first woman I've felt an attraction for since Caroline's been gone." He rested his forearms on the table and leaned forward. "I have been thinking about inviting her to the Harvest Ball. Do you think I should ask her?"

Mac gave his question some thought before answering. "I don't see no reason fer you not to ask her."

"Do you think I should see what Carrie thinks first?"

"I kin tell you right now the little lady ain't goin' to like it. Not one little bit."

"Maybe I should forget the whole idea."

"You shouldn't do no sich thing." Mac gathered up their cups and limped to the sink. "Me an' Cyrus is gettin' up in years.

We ain't gonna be here ferever, you know."

Sherman drew himself up to protest, but Mac cut him off before he could speak. "It's the way it's meant to be. Ever'thing dies in due season." He resumed his seat across from Sherman. "The little lady got her own family now. Someday she'll have young 'uns that will take up her time. Life kin get mighty lonely, Sherm. Miz Casey's a fine woman. But her an' thet little Hope is a lot alike. They've both been hurt real bad. If yer wantin' to win her heart yer gonna have to be mighty patient."

"Right now I only want to become better acquainted with her."

"Then you ast her to that ball, and if she says no jist don't give up. An' another thing, Sherm, don't worry none 'bout what the little lady thinks. I don't reckon she's gonna be too happy if she thinks someone else might take her place in yer affections, but she'll get over it."

"No one could ever take Carrie's place, Mac. You know that."

"Course not. Ever'one's got their own spot. The little lady may not realize thet yet." Mac scratched his chin with a gnarled forefinger. "We spoiled Carrie rotten, Sherm, but we never raised her to be selfish. If somethin' should come of yore friendship with Miz Casey, it might take awhile, but she'll come round."

❧

Sherman tried to catch Mariah's eye at services the following Sunday, but she kept her head turned away from him. After the meeting ended he headed in her direction, but Emily James intercepted him. By the time he was able to escape the Widow James, Mariah had left with Tom and Joanna Brady. He thought about stopping by her house on the way home and inviting her to the ball but decided it wouldn't be seemly to call on a lady who lived alone.

❧

For the first time in her life women stopped Mariah on the

street to chat about their children. They exchanged recipes and childcare tips. Despite the difference in their ages, she developed an especially close friendship with Joanna Brady.

Hope was a constant delight. Mariah had never felt more fulfilled as a woman. Yet every time she saw Carrie Nolan or her father, her stomach twisted with shame. She tried to avoid them—father and daughter—as much as possible. Carrie maintained her distance, barely acknowledging Mariah's existence. Sherman, however, was a different story. Several times Mariah barely escaped an encounter with him at church.

One Saturday afternoon in mid-October, Joanna Brady came calling. "It's such a beautiful fall day, I decided to go for a walk," she said, after Mariah invited her into the kitchen and put the teapot on. "Before I knew it, I was knocking on your front door."

"I'm so happy you stopped by," Mariah said. "Hope is taking a nap, and I was baking cookies. Oatmeal. They are her favorite."

"Mine, too." Joanna took a seat at the kitchen table.

"The last panful is about ready to come out of the oven." Mariah put several warm cookies on a plate and set them on the table. "Help yourself."

As soon as she removed the final pan of cookies from the oven, she poured them each a cup of tea and sat down across from Joanna.

Joanna stirred her tea before lifting the cup for a dainty sip. "This is the best tea I've ever tasted, Mariah. Wherever did you get it?"

"I blend my own." Mariah blushed at the compliment. "I'm glad you like it."

"I like it very much. You are an absolute wonder, Mariah." She set her cup down and helped herself to another cookie. "How is Hope doing?"

"Quite well." Mariah stirred a teaspoon of sugar into her

tea. "She's extremely bright."

"Spoken like a doting mother," Joanna teased.

"I still have trouble believing God has given me this beautiful little girl," Mariah said. "I always dreamed of a large family. Of course it never happened."

"It still might."

"It's too late now. Besides, Hope is enough. I feel very blessed to have her."

"Hope is very blessed to have you. You are a wonderful mother, Mariah."

Mariah had received few compliments in her life and found Joanna's comments disconcerting. To cover her confusion she refilled Joanna's cup, then resumed her seat across the table from the younger woman. "I want to be a good mother more than anything in this world," she confessed, "but I fear I have no idea how to begin."

"Nonsense." Joanna smiled. "It's instinctive. God created women to be nurturing. Keepers of the flame, my father says."

"Not all women have that instinct." Mariah looked at the sweet-faced girl sitting across the table from her. Joanna was the only close friend she had ever had. In the short time she had lived in Cedar Bend she had come to love her. Now she trusted her with the dark secret of her heart. "My mother despised me."

"Oh no! That can't be true." Sympathy darkened the girl's eyes, and she reached out to cover Mariah's hand with hers. "I'm so sorry, Mariah."

"She never wanted me. I was a cruel disappointment to her. Those are her words, not mine." Mariah shrugged her shoulders. "It doesn't really matter."

"Of course it matters." Joanna's dark eyes filled with tears. "I'm so sorry for your pain."

"She never touched me when I was small. Never put her arms around me. Never read me a bedtime story. Never came

when I was frightened and cried out for her in the night."
Tears came to Mariah's blue eyes and rolled down her cheeks.
"How can I be a good mother when I never had a mother?"

"Do you love Hope?"

"More than anything in this world."

"Do you read her a bedtime story and tuck her in at night?"
At Mariah's affirmative nod Joanna continued. "If she was
frightened would you go to her?"

Mariah blotted her tears with a napkin. "I would give my
life for her."

"I know you would." Joanna squeezed Mariah's hand.
"Because you are her mother. Don't you feel like just squeezing
the stuffing out of her?"

A faint smile lifted the corners of Mariah's mouth. "Sometimes it takes all my willpower to keep from scooping her up
and hugging her."

"Why don't you?"

Mariah's smile faded as she looked deep into her own heart
and soul. She raised her head and met Joanna's gentle gaze.
"I'm afraid she will push me away."

"Did your mother push you away?"

Mariah nodded. "She didn't like to be mussed."

"What about your father?"

Mariah took a sip from her blue-flowered mug before
answering. "Father had his church. His 'flock' he called them.
They kept him busy. I know he cared for me, but there was
always someone seeking his guidance."

"You know, Mariah, you are going to have to take the
risk of reaching out." Joanna's dark eyes were serious. "Some
people may reject you. That is the way life is. Most will accept
you if only you stop holding them at arm's length. Except for
church and the occasional Sunday dinner with us you never
socialize. Why is that, Mariah?"

"I'm reserved like my father," Mariah said.

"I'm sure your father was dignified," Joanna replied. "That is how I visualize him. Stately, and very dignified. But he certainly wasn't reserved. He reached out to people."

"Father was a good shepherd. Everyone adored him."

"The people of Cedar Bend think highly of you, Mariah. They are eager to love you if only you'll allow them to." A sudden smile brightened Joanna's face. "I have a wonderful idea. It's time you were presented to society."

Presented to society! Mariah felt like a character in a romance as Joanna chattered on about what she must wear and how they could do her hair. Finally she held up a hand to stop the stream of words. "Don't you think I'm a bit old for all this? And besides, where did you plan for this unveiling to take place?"

"You aren't old, Mariah. My goodness, I hope I have a complexion like yours when I'm your age. You don't have a single wrinkle. The Harvest Ball is next Saturday night. I know you are a wonderful seamstress. Can you have a dress finished by then?"

"I have nothing from which to make a dress."

"We have plenty of time to walk to the mercantile and buy fabric, notions, everything you need. I'll help with the cutting and basting. Oh, Mariah, this will be such fun."

Joanna's enthusiasm was contagious. Mariah found herself almost believing that she could live her own version of Cinderella. Then reality settled in. She was a thirty-six-year-old spinster. Even if she went to the ball there would be no Prince Charming for her. No happily ever after.

"I'm afraid it's too late," she murmured.

"Nonsense." Joanna glanced at the clock on the shelf, then pushed her chair back and stood. "It isn't even two o'clock yet. Take off your apron, put on your bonnet, and let's go."

"I'd like to, Joanna," Mariah said. In a way it was the truth. Going shopping with Joanna, making the dress together that would transform her into the belle of the ball, it all sounded like such fun. Fun to think about but unrealistic. It was a relief to add, "But Hope is sleeping."

"Wake her up."

"I couldn't do that. Hope's naptime is very important to her."

Joanna sat back down. "Maybe she will wake up in a few minutes."

"Probably not. She only fell asleep shortly before you came. She will probably sleep a couple of hours."

Five minutes later Hope padded into the kitchen looking bright-eyed, rosy-cheeked, and positively adorable. "No more excuses." Joanna hugged Hope. "I'll put on her shoes while you get ready."

Mariah sighed as she untied her apron. "I can't go to this ball alone."

"Of course not. You're going with us. Daddy told me to invite you." Joanna took Hope's hand and led her from the room.

❧

Mariah couldn't remember ever spending a more enjoyable afternoon. Joanna and Mrs. Harris insisted the deep rose-colored brocade the mercantile had received in its last shipment was perfect for her. When she protested that she was thinking more on the line of a serviceable gray, Joanna and Mrs. Harris shook their heads.

Back at Mariah's house the two women cut out and basted the rose-colored fabric. When Mariah tried on the basted bodice, Joanna studied her closely, then declared she looked lovely.

Mariah blushed when she saw her image in the bedroom mirror. The rose—while not something she would have chosen for herself—did bring color to her cheeks. Still, she could see nothing lovely in her appearance. "No matter what I wear I look like a mop stick."

"You are tall and elegant like Snow White." Joanna giggled.

"I, on the other hand, look like one of your dwarfs. Hope, don't you think your mama looks like a princess?"

The little girl, who was sitting on Mariah's bed watching the goings on with wide eyes, nodded.

"Mama is going to be the belle of the ball, isn't she?"

Once more Hope nodded.

"Prince Charming will walk in the door. His blue eyes will scan the room. He will see a lovely lady dressed in rose. *Who is this beautiful stranger?* His heart will skip a beat. He will cross the room to where she is sitting. Bowing low before her, he will extend his hand and ask her to dance."

Joanna pantomimed her words. She scanned the room until her gaze rested on Hope; then she gasped and put a hand to her heart. She crossed the room to the bed and bowed in front of the child. "May I have this dance, beautiful stranger?"

Giggling, Hope slid from the bed and placed her tiny hand in Joanna's hand. Mariah sank into a chair and watched as Joanna waltzed around the room with Hope. Finally both girls collapsed onto the bed laughing until they were breathless. Mariah, still sitting in her grandmother's rocking chair, laughed with them until tears rolled down her cheeks.

ten

Time was running out. Since the afternoon Mariah and Hope spent at the Circle C, Mariah had avoided Sherman like the plague. Several times he tried to approach her after church only to be intercepted by someone. By the time he was free, she had vanished. As he rode to church Sherman determined this Sunday was going to be different. With less than a week remaining until the Harvest Ball, he was going to corner Mariah Casey and invite her to the fall gathering.

Sherman sat in the last pew instead of his accustomed seat. As soon as the final prayer was said and the service was dismissed, Mariah and Hope headed for the door. He remained in his seat until the last possible moment before stepping into the aisle, effectively blocking her exit.

"Miss Casey, I would like a word with you."

She reminded him of a cornered deer as her eyes darted from one side to the other looking for a means of escape. Finding no way out, she exhaled, and her shoulders slumped. "Mr. Butler, I am in a hurry. Sunday dinner is in the oven, and I have guests coming." Her eyes were fixed on his shirtfront. "May we please pass?"

"Not until you tell me what is wrong. What have I done to offend you?" He wanted to reach out and cup her chin in his hand. Force her eyes to meet his. "I had such an enjoyable afternoon the Sunday you came to the ranch for dinner. I thought you did, too."

For the briefest moment her eyes met his, and he saw the sheen of tears before she dropped her gaze. "I really must go, Mr. Butler. Joanna is waiting."

"If you would only allow me a moment. I wanted to ask you—"

"Papa, there you are." Carrie slipped her arm through his. "Hello, Miss Casey. Dr. Brady is waiting for you."

A crimson flush swept up Mariah's neck and stained her alabaster skin all the way to her hairline. Without a word she scooped Hope up, slipped past Sherman and Carrie, and hurried from the building.

"Well," Carrie remarked, "that certainly wasn't very polite. She never even spoke to me."

"Something is bothering her," Sherman said. "I only wish I knew what it was."

"Hmm," Carrie murmured as they stepped from the church into the sunny October afternoon. "Guess what Joanna told me? Her father is escorting Miss Casey to the Harvest Ball. You may lose your teacher after all, Papa."

Sherman stopped dead in his tracks. "Tom is escorting Miss Casey?" A keen sense of disappointment washed over him.

"I think from what I've been told it's quite serious," Carrie said as he handed her into the buggy beside Lucas.

"Quite serious." Carrie's words echoed in his head as he rode to the Circle C. Sherman Butler wasn't one to give up without a fight, but Tom Brady was his friend. It was Tom who had seen Caroline through her final illness. If Tom were interested in Mariah, he would respect their friendship and not muddy the waters by pressing his own suit.

❧

Saturday afternoon Joanna appeared at Mariah's front door carrying a small black case. "Whatever are you doing here?" Mariah asked. She then added, "Not that I'm not happy to see you. It's only that I wasn't expecting you."

"I'm your fairy godmother, Cinderella." Joanna giggled. "I have my bag of magic to transform you."

"We are Christians, Joanna." Mariah frowned. "We don't

believe in fairy godmothers or magic."

"I know we don't," Joanna agreed with a smile. "However, we do believe in transformations."

"Of the heart and soul," Mariah said. "Not of plain looks and dull features."

"Nonsense," Joanna scoffed. "You're beautiful as God made you. We are just going to emphasize that beauty. It's time you quit hiding your light under a bushel, Mariah. Now, shall we draw milady's bath?"

"Fine." Mariah laughed. There was something about Joanna's perpetual optimism that made her feel young and giddy. "You are about to discover you can't make a silk purse out of a sow's ear."

While Joanna entertained Hope in the living room, Mariah bathed in the kitchen. She felt positively decadent lounging in a hot tub in the middle of the afternoon. Mother would be horrified. The scent of lilac drifted up from the water. It smelled wonderful. *I don't care what Mother would think. I was a dutiful daughter while she was alive. Now, under God's guidance, I must be the mistress of my own destiny.* The warm water was so relaxing, her eyes drifted shut.

More asleep than awake, she imagined herself walking into the social hall of the Cattlemen's Association on Sherman Butler's arm. Everyone in the room turned to smile at her. She saw the affection in their expressions and knew they were her friends. Even Carrie Nolan smiled a greeting.

Mariah's eyes popped open. "Forevermore, Mariah Casey, have you taken complete leave of your senses?" She thought of Sherman Butler paying her court, and she thought of the way Carrie smiled at her in her dream with genuine affection. "When pigs fly," she muttered to herself.

❧

Freshly bathed, dusted with lilac bath powder, and wearing her ratty old dressing gown, Mariah sat in front of her vanity mirror with Hope leaning against her knee.

"The first thing we are going to do is get rid of that bun," Joanna said.

Mariah's hands flew to the bun at the back of her head. "I've worn it this way since I was old enough to put my hair up."

"All the more reason to change it." Joanna began to remove hairpins. "Don't you agree, Hope?"

The little girl who was watching the proceedings in wide-eyed interest nodded her head in vigorous agreement.

"You two are impossible." Mariah smiled. She rested a hand on Hope's head. The first thing she had done after Hope came to live with her was get rid of those painfully tight braids. Now, except at night when her hair was loosely braided to keep it from tangling, Hope had ringlets that reached to her waist. Maybe it was time she changed her own hairstyle. When the last pin was removed, Mariah's hair tumbled around her shoulders.

Joanna had only been brushing a short while when she laughed.

Mariah glanced in the mirror to make sure her hair wasn't all falling out. It wasn't. "What's wrong?"

"It's your hair. The more I brush, the curlier it gets."

"I know," Mariah sighed. "Mother said it looked like sheep's wool. That's why I always wore it pulled back so tightly."

"It most certainly does not look like sheep's wool," Joanna huffed. "It's almost exactly like Hope's. Do you think her hair looks like sheep's wool?"

"Of course not." Mariah ran a gentle hand over the little girl's loose ringlets. "Hope has beautiful hair."

"And so do you." She stepped back and cocked her head to one side, studying Mariah intently. "Mmm," she murmured. "Mmm-hmm." She moved slightly to study her from a different angle. After about the sixth "Mmm-hmm," Mariah began to get nervous.

"I know it's hopeless." Her slender shoulders slumped. "Why not forget the whole thing and fix it like I've always worn it."

"Hopeless! *Au contraire, mademoiselle.*"

"Joanna, I didn't know you spoke French."

Joanna giggled. "You have heard my entire French vocabulary. I believe I read those words in a romance novel Mac loaned me."

"Mr. McDougal? He reads romance novels?"

"Indeed he does. Mac is an avid reader."

Mariah shook her head in wonder. If she had taken time to think about it, which she hadn't, she would have assumed the kindly little man was illiterate.

"That's what makes people so interesting, Mariah. Everyone has little things nobody knows about them."

"Do you have a secret, Joanna?" Mariah teased.

"No, my life is an open book." Joanna grinned at Mariah's reflection in the mirror. "Except for one thing."

Mariah, intrigued despite herself, couldn't resist asking, "What deep, dark secret are you hiding, Joanna?"

Joanna picked up the brush and ran it through Mariah's hair. "I'll tell you my secret if you'll tell me yours."

Mariah had been a shy, awkward child who had grown up to be a shy, reticent woman. She had never been close to anyone, but in spite of the difference in their ages she and Joanna had come to be close friends. She had a lifetime of confidences stored up. Which one could she share?

"It doesn't have to be anything embarrassing," Joanna prodded. "Well, not too embarrassing anyway."

Mariah thought of the beauty cream she had bought so many years ago. At the time it seemed tragic. Now in retrospect it was rather amusing. She was sure Joanna would enjoy it. "All right, I have one. When I was sixteen I realized I was never going to be pretty. At least not without help."

Joanna shook her head as if to argue, and Hope leaned comfortingly against Mariah. She continued, "So I saved my money and bought some beauty cream."

"Oh, Mariah, you didn't need that." Joanna slapped a hand over her mouth to stifle a giggle. "Did you notice any change?"

"Not really. I used it faithfully every night for months. Mother was snooping through my things one day while I was at school and found it. She was waiting for me when I got home. That was the end of the beauty cream."

"Your mother made you throw it away?"

"Mother had a temper and a tongue that could cut a person to shreds." Remembering the horrible, hurtful things her mother had said to her that long-ago day brought a rush of tears to Mariah's eyes. She quickly blinked them away, but not quickly enough.

Sympathetic tears filled Joanna's dark eyes. "I'm sorry, Mariah." She put her arms around Mariah's shoulders and hugged her tight.

Hope laid her head in Mariah's lap and patted her leg. "I sorry, Mama."

"Joanna, did you hear that?" Mariah scooped the little girl up into her arms and hugged her. "Hope, you can talk! I knew you could."

Joanna's smile was so bright it seemed to light up the room. "Aren't you something, young lady! You had a better secret than either your mama or me."

When the two women tried to persuade Hope to speak again, she hid her face against Mariah's neck and shook her head.

"At least we know she can when she wants to," Mariah said. "Although I am a bit disappointed."

"Don't be." Joanna patted the little girl's ebony curls. "I have a feeling once she starts talking, she won't stop. Besides, we've witnessed a miracle today."

"Of course we have," Mariah agreed. "Hope did speak and will again."

"True." Joanna grinned. "However, that isn't the miracle I was referring to. What are you doing, Mariah?"

Mariah's face was a study in confusion as she looked up at Joanna. Then the light of understanding brightened her features. She mouthed the words, "Hugging Hope."

"And what is Hope doing?" Joanna whispered in return.

The little girl's arms were wrapped tightly around Mariah's neck. She had reached out to Hope, and Hope hadn't pushed her away. The woman rested her cheek against the little girl's curls.

"Hope, you are going to have to sit on the bed and watch while I do your mama's hair. Okay?"

"Okay," Hope parroted as Mariah reluctantly released her. She slid off Mariah's lap and ran and climbed up on the bed.

Joy washed over Mariah as her heart struggled to break free of the walls that had imprisoned it for so many years. She felt as if she could soar right up to heaven. She wanted to sing and dance and praise the Lord. Since she only knew how to do one of the three, she whispered a prayer of thanksgiving to God for sending Hope and Joanna into her life.

"I have decided to give you a fringe." Joanna interrupted her prayer, bringing her back to earth with a thud.

"A fringe?" She noticed her friend had produced a pair of scissors from somewhere. "You mean cut my hair?" Mariah wrapped both arms around her head to protect her hair from the gleaming, extremely sharp-looking instrument in the girl's hand. "No. No. No, Joanna! I have never had scissors touch my hair."

"Don't be such a baby. A fringe will be very becoming." Joanna took hold of one of Mariah's arms and gently drew it down. "This won't hurt a bit."

"Isn't that what Delilah said to Samson?"

Joanna giggled. "You are a very witty person when you let your hair down. Now sit still."

When Joanna parted off and combed a thin layer of hair down over her face, Mariah closed her eyes. When she felt the cold steel of the scissors against her forehead she moaned. At the first cut, she whimpered softly. She held any other sounds back until she felt Joanna stop.

"Very nice," Joanna said.

Mariah opened her eyes a slit and took a peek. It didn't look bad. She opened her eyes all the way. Joanna lay down the scissors and went to work in earnest. Ten minutes later she nodded in satisfaction. "There! What do you think?"

The fringe and the short, wispy curls that surrounded her face softened the angles. She picked the hand mirror up from the vanity and turned so she could see the back. Her hair was a mass of elaborately pinned-in curls high on the back of her head.

Hope padded across the room and gently touched the fringe of hair on Mariah's forehead. "Pretty," she said.

Two warm tears rolled down Mariah's cheeks. "Thank you," she whispered.

"You are quite welcome." Joanna leaned down and kissed her forehead. "There's only one more thing before I leave. She reached into her bag and produced a small, squat jar. "A touch of this and you will be perfect."

"Face paint?" Mariah cringed. "I can't wear face paint. I'm a schoolteacher. Whatever will people think?"

"It's only a bit of rouge. No one will even know you have it on. Trust me." She added with a giggle, "It's not like it's beauty cream."

Mariah smiled and sighed in defeat. She allowed Joanna to add a bit of color to her cheeks and her lips. When Joanna was finished and Mariah turned back to the mirror, she could scarcely believe the transformation. Her face seemed to have come alive. Even her eyes had a sparkle that had never been there before.

Joanna was returning items to her bag. "You are all done except for putting on your dress. I'm going home to get ready. We will pick you up at six thirty." She stooped to kiss Hope. "Bye, sweetheart. See you later."

"Bye, sweethot. See ya lateah," the little girl said.

"My goodness." The young woman smiled. "You are becoming a regular chatterbox. Mariah, you know the old saying about little pitchers having big ears. We are going to have to start watching what we say around you-know-who. Our secrets may become town gossip."

"Speaking of secrets," Mariah said. "You never did tell me yours."

"Remember I told you about Clay Shepherd? The boy whose father was a drifter?"

Mariah nodded. "Yes, I remember. He left town right after you graduated from the eighth grade."

"We went early to the Christmas play practice. No one else was there. Clay kissed me underneath the mistletoe. That was my first, last, and only kiss from a boy." Joanna sighed and put a hand to her cheek, as if that long-ago kiss still remained there. "I was smitten. Isn't that silly?"

"I don't think so." Mariah escorted her friend to the door. "I think it was rather forward of young Master Shepherd, but I also think it is sweet."

"Clay liked Carrie a lot, but she steered a wide path around him. He was wild, and she said he was dangerous. Carrie was right about him, I suppose." Joanna sighed. "If I'd had a lick of sense I would probably have been afraid of him, too. But he was incredibly handsome, and without doubt the most exciting male I had ever met."

Mariah smiled sympathetically, but she thought it was a

good thing that Clay Shepherd had left town before he broke her friend's heart.

She watched Joanna walk down the street, then closed the door and leaned against it for a moment. She had a friend to share confidences with. Hope could speak. No matter what happened at the Harvest Ball, this would still be the most perfect day of her entire life.

eleven

Sherman Butler felt a small catch in his chest when he saw Mariah step through the door of the Cattlemen's Association meeting hall with Hope clinging to her hand. There was something different about her hair, and she was wearing a rose-colored dress. She stood straight and tall as she gazed around the room. That was one of the things that attracted him to her. Most tall women slumped in an effort to look shorter. Not Mariah. She was tall, proud, graceful, and beautiful. Her eyes meet his, then quickly shifted away.

While he watched, a group of chattering women surrounded Mariah and Joanna. Tom walked away to visit with one of the local ranchers. Then Carrie and Lucas arrived. With his daughter clinging to his side, Sherman forced his attention from Mariah.

&

Mariah saw Mr. Sherman Butler as soon as she stepped through the door of the meeting hall. Her eyes met his before she managed to look away. His daughter and son-in-law arrived shortly after that. Carrie was wearing a sparkling, emerald green dress that accentuated her auburn hair and flawless skin. She immediately took possession of her father, urging him toward the punch bowl.

Mariah tried not to look at them, but they were difficult to avoid. Even if Mr. Butler hadn't been the tallest man in the room, his and Carrie's copper-colored hair shone forth like beacons, distinguishing them from the crowd. She forced her mind away from the Butler family as a steady stream of her students and their mothers surged around to greet her.

Her cousin, Lucille Smith, and Lucille's friend, Gretchen Racine, rushed over to compliment Mariah's dress and becoming hairstyle. "Oh, Cousin Mariah, you look divine! I wish Mama could see you." Lucille rolled her big, green eyes. "Mama insisted on staying home with her grandson tonight. She practically forced Jed and me out of the house." She sighed dramatically and leaned close to Mariah. "She will be so happy when I tell her that I saw you tonight. Mama keeps saying that Kansas has been so good for you."

Kansas had indeed been good for her. Mariah smiled warmly. "Tell Cousin Gladys that Hope and I will stop in to see her soon."

For the next hour the friendly crowd mingled and visited as people gathered around the refreshment table. Promptly at eight o'clock the floor was cleared for the dance. This was the part of the evening Mariah most dreaded. She took a seat in one of the chairs that had been pushed back against the wall. Joanna sat on one side of her with Hope on the other, while the fiddler warmed up on a raised platform at the end of the room.

A tall, slender man Mariah recognized as the father of one of her first graders stepped up onto the platform. "Everybody choose your partner for the first set," he announced.

Little Karl Braun came over and asked Hope if she would be his partner. Mariah looked into her daughter's pleading eyes and nodded her permission. L. K. took Hope's hand, and the two of them skipped across the room to join a group of children.

"Well," Joanna said, "now I really feel like a wallflower."

"Little Karl always treats Hope so well."

Joanna laughed. "I declare, Mariah. You'll be making Hope's wedding gown before you make mine."

"Don't be silly, Joanna. Hope is only a baby." Mariah was watching the two children and didn't realize that Mark Hopkins had approached until she heard him ask Joanna to dance.

"Would you mind, Mariah?" Joanna's voice held a hint of apology. "I hate to leave you here alone."

Mariah turned her attention to the young couple. "Nonsense. Go ahead and have a good time. I'll be fine."

As soon as Joanna and Mark left, Tom Brady sat down beside Mariah. "Are you sure you wouldn't like to dance, Miss Casey?"

Before Mariah had time to reply, the fiddle player began a sprightly tune accompanied by the caller. The noise rendered conversation impossible. Both Mariah and the doctor turned their attention to the dancers who were divided into sets of eight.

"Choose your partner," Mr. Cox called out in a singsong rhythm. "Form a ring. Figure eight, and double-L swing."

The man certainly had a set of lungs on him. No wonder little Ezra Cox was so loud and rambunctious.

"Swing 'em once and let 'em go," Mr. Cox sang out. "All hands left and do-si-do."

Across the room Hope's dark curls bounced as L. K. swung her around. The tiny girl smiled up at her husky blond partner, and Mariah had a heart-wrenching vision of the future. She imagined her little girl as a beautiful, petite young woman with gleaming ebony curls smiling up at her burly, blond companion. She closed her eyes and shook her head slightly to clear her mind. *Goodness, Mariah,* she silently chided herself, *you know Joanna is only teasing. Besides, you want Hope to grow up and have beaux, and someday you want her to marry and have babies.*

"How will you swap?" Mr. Cox sang out, "And how'll you trade?"

She opened her eyes and saw that the children were changing partners.

"This pretty girl for the old maid?"

I certainly don't want her to be a lonely, old maid schoolteacher. Mariah's mouth twisted. *I'm not ready to lose her either. But that's years in the future.*

She felt a hand on her arm and turned her head to see concern in the doctor's dark eyes. He leaned over and spoke against her ear. "Are you all right?"

Mariah nodded in reply. "I'm fine," she mouthed to him.

He smiled and turned his attention back to the dancers, his foot tapping in time with the music. She scanned the room until her gaze came to rest on an auburn-haired man who stood head and shoulders above everyone else in the room. He was leaning against the wall, talking to Mr. Harris. She seized the opportunity to study him closely while his attention was elsewhere. He looked her direction, and she shifted her gaze to the children.

As soon as the final note of the fiddle faded away, the laughing dancers descended on the refreshment table for a glass of apple cider. When the caller announced the second set, Mariah insisted Dr. Brady join the dancers. He gave a token argument before asking the Widow James to be his partner.

Mac McDougal hobbled over and sat down in his unoccupied chair. "You look mighty purty tonight, Mariah."

She couldn't control the pleasurable glow that crept up her neck and assuredly stained her cheeks. "Thank you, Mac. I'm glad you think so."

"I ain't a flatterer, young lady. Yer a mighty purty woman, and I ain't the only one thet thinks so. How come yer feller is gettin' ready to dance with the widder 'stead of sittin' here with you?"

"My fellow?" Mariah's cheeks blazed. "What fellow? I don't have a—whatever are you talking about?"

"I heerd you an' the doc was courtin'. Ain't you?"

"The doc? You mean Dr. Brady?" Mariah put her hands to her burning cheeks. How many people besides Mac had heard that she was keeping company with Tom Brady? "I don't know who told you that Dr. Brady and I were—" She was so embarrassed she couldn't even bring herself to say the word. "It's not true. I never even thought of him as—"

"Then you an' him ain't courtin'?" Mac's faded blue eyes twinkled.

"Of course not," Mariah insisted. "I consider Dr. Brady a friend. That's all."

"I know somebody thet's gonna be mighty happy to hear thet," Mac murmured as the fiddle began to play another sprightly tune that almost drowned out his voice. "An' I know a young lady thet's gonna have a mite of explainin' to do when I get my hands on her."

The fiddle and Levi Cox's calling made further conversation impossible. Mariah turned her attention to Hope. Her tiny daughter was laughing as she skipped around a circle with the other children. The wonder that this child was hers brought a smile to Mariah's heart. So what if an absurd rumor was circulating about her and Tom Brady? Today, for the first time, Hope had called her *Mama*.

♦

Sherman Butler watched Mariah from across the room. Her eyes were on the children, and there was a radiance about her that tore at his heart. He scanned the dancers until he found Tom Brady and Emily James, and his eyes narrowed. Everyone in town knew the widow was looking to replace her late husband. Why on earth would his friend want to spend his time with Mrs. James when he was courting the finest woman in town? *Maybe he isn't keeping company with Miss Casey.* The thought brought a sudden surge of hope. *Maybe Carrie misunderstood.*

As soon as the set ended, he approached Tom Brady and the widow. "I need to speak to you, Tom."

"Let me fill Mrs. James's glass first."

The widow dabbed at her flushed cheeks with a lace-trimmed handkerchief while the doctor filled her glass at the refreshment table. "I haven't noticed you dancing, Mr. Butler."

"I rarely dance, Mrs. James."

"What a shame." She rested a small hand on his arm. "You move so gracefully for such a tall man. I'm sure you are a wonderful dancer."

Sherman had met many women like the Widow James since Caroline passed away. Women who looked at a man with desperate eyes. Women who clung to a man's arm with all the tenacity of a drowning victim. He looked down at the rough, work-worn hand resting on his sleeve, and an unexpected wave of compassion washed over him. It must be frightening for a woman to be left suddenly alone with three half-grown children and a hardscrabble farm.

"Thank you, Mrs. James, but I'm afraid I'm not much of a dancer."

"Perhaps you haven't found the right partner."

Her eyes held a hint of sorrow, and Sherman thought she looked tired. His gaze drifted to Mariah sitting against the wall, talking to Mac. The widow was wrong. He had found the right partner. He only hoped he hadn't waited too long to declare himself.

"Here you are." Tom Brady pressed a chilled glass into the widow's hand. "Now, what can I do for you, Sherm?"

"I'd like to speak to you for a moment." He glanced at the woman sipping cider. "Alone if you don't mind."

"Certainly. Please excuse me, Mrs. James, and thank you for the dance."

Sherman led the doctor through the milling crowd and out

the side door into a deserted alley. After a few steps he turned to his friend. "Tom, I want to know what your intentions are concerning Miss Casey."

"Miss Casey? The schoolteacher? Joanna's friend? I have no intentions regarding her. Why would you ask such a question, Sherm?"

"I just—" The big man ran his fingers through his hair. "I heard—someone told me—that you were courting the teacher. That it was serious."

"Well, someone was mistaken. I like Mariah Casey. She's an asset to our community. But no, I am not courting her."

A flood of relief washed over Sherman, bringing a smile to his face. "Are you seeing her home tonight?"

"Joanna and I are supposed to." The doctor cocked his head to one side. "Are you interested in Miss Casey?"

Sherman cleared his throat. "I might be."

"Why don't you speak up? Ask her if you can come calling."

"I would if she'd give me a chance. Tom, she runs from me like I was contagious."

"Mariah Casey is reserved, but I haven't found her to be unfriendly. If we put our heads together maybe we can come up with a way for the two of you to get better acquainted."

❧

The last dance was being called when Mariah saw Joanna and her father talking to Sherman Butler. She hadn't seen either man for some time. Not that she'd been looking for them. It was only that they were conspicuous by their absence.

Hope, who was sleeping with her head cradled in Mariah's lap, stirred. She brushed the little girl's tousled curls back from her forehead and felt another crack in the hard shell that had enclosed her heart for so many years. *Thank You, Lord, for giving this precious child into my care. Help me to be the mother she deserves, and, Lord, give me the strength to become the woman You would have me to be. Help me dwell on whatever things are pure and lovely. Help me to be open and kind to everyone.*

When she looked up the Bradys were nowhere in sight, and Sherman Butler was heading her way. Her stomach flip-flopped at the sight of the handsome rancher, and she added a hasty postscript to her prayer. *Dear Father, please help me to remember who I am and take away the feelings I have for Mr. Butler.*

"Miss Casey, Tom and Joanna had to leave unexpectedly—you know how it is with doctors—and they asked me to see you and Hope home."

For a moment Mariah felt as if all her dreams were coming true; then reality raised its ugly head. Mr. Butler might be—not *might* be—he *was* the most handsome man at the ball, but she was most certainly not Cinderella. She was a homely, middle-aged spinster schoolteacher whose foot would never fit a dainty glass slipper.

"You are ready to leave, aren't you?" Not waiting for her reply he leaned down and scooped Hope up. The little girl settled down against his chest, rested her head against his broad shoulder, and snuggled her face into his neck. Holding her with one arm, he reached his free hand to Mariah.

Ignoring his offer of assistance, Mariah rose. She had sat so long with Hope's head in her lap that her left foot and leg were asleep. Pins and needles shot from her foot to her knee, causing her to stumble. Immediately his hand was on her elbow, steadying her. "Careful there."

"I'm fine." She shook off his hand. "It is kind of you to offer to see us home, but it's only a few blocks. We'll walk."

"I have my horse so you'll have to walk." His dimples flashed. "But you aren't walking alone. I'm walking with you."

"It's kind of you to offer, but we will be fine. Now if you will just give Hope to me—" She put her hands on the little girl's waist and tried to lift her away from him. Hope murmured a few unintelligible words and slipped both arms around the man's neck, clinging even tighter.

"Hey!" A delighted grin spread across his face. "I didn't know she was talking. When did she start?"

"Today." For a moment Mariah forgot everything but the thrill of Hope's few spoken words. "She didn't say much, but what she did say was clear."

Mariah didn't see Carrie approaching, but suddenly she was there. "Papa, whatever are you doing?"

"The Bradys had to leave unexpectedly, and I'm going to escort Miss Casey home."

His smile was met by a frown. "You didn't bring a buggy."

Mariah knew that Carrie thought she was a desperate old maid who was out to snag her father. The young woman had made that clear when she showed her the portrait of her mother. Humiliation was no stranger to Mariah. She had been demeaned and mocked most of her life. Still, it hurt. She wished she could grab Hope and vanish.

"If you give me Hope, we'll leave." Mariah put her hand on the child. "It isn't far, and no one will harm us."

"You aren't walking home by yourself. I promised I would see you safely home, and that is what I'm going to do."

Mariah was beginning to realize Sherman Butler had a stubborn streak.

"Nonsense," Carrie snapped. "We will see her home."

So did his daughter.

"No!" The single word escaped before Mariah could stop it. She would walk a mile over hot coals before she would get into another buggy with Carrie Nolan.

Lucas Nolan had been standing quietly to one side. Now he put his arm around his wife's shoulders. "It's a warm night and there's a full moon. A moonlight stroll sounds like a good idea to me."

"Moonlight stroll!" Carrie sputtered. "No, it's not a good idea."

"Course it is, darlin'." He began to ease his wife away from them. "Good night, Miss Casey. Sherm. See you at church tomorrow."

Mariah was almost sure she saw Lucas wink at Mr. Butler as he led Carrie away.

twelve

Mariah took off like she was going to a fire, only slowing her steps when Sherman made it obvious he didn't plan on being hurried. They walked in silence for a time, Sherman cradling Hope in one arm and leading his horse with the other hand, Mariah at his side.

Her profile was clear in the light of the full moon. Sherman wanted to know more about this woman he found so appealing. He cleared his throat. "Has it been difficult for you to adjust to life on the Kansas prairie?"

Mariah kept her gaze straight ahead. "Not at all."

"You don't miss Ohio then?"

"No."

"You never consider going back?"

"Had there been anything for me in Ohio I wouldn't have come here."

"You lived there your whole life. Surely you have friends that you want to see again. You must get homesick."

She turned her head to look at him. "I never had friends, Mr. Butler."

"In the short time that you have been here you've made a host of friends."

She turned her face away from him. "It's different here. I'm different."

He wanted to ask in what way she was different but felt it would be presumptuous to do so. "It's a beautiful night, isn't it?"

"Yes, it is." She pulled her shawl a bit tighter around her shoulders. "A bit chilly, perhaps." She lifted her face to the harvest moon. "I suppose that's to be expected this time of year."

Hope snuggled closer and burrowed her face into his neck. "I've seen some bad blizzards in October," he said.

"Yes. Cousin Gladys told me that the weather can be unpredictable."

Sooner than he would have liked, they were walking up the steps to Mariah's front porch. At the door she turned to face him. "Thank you for seeing us home, Mr. Butler. I'll take Hope now."

Sherman reluctantly released the little girl into Mariah's arms. "Before you go in, Miss Casey, there is something I would like to ask you."

He couldn't see her face in the shadows, but he felt her blue eyes on him. Beautiful blue eyes. He felt as shy as a boy with his first girl. Taking a deep breath, he plunged in. "I was wondering—that is, I thought—" This was more difficult than he remembered. He took a deep breath and slowly exhaled. "Would you and Hope come out to the Circle C for dinner tomorrow? After church, I mean."

Mariah's hesitation was a palpable thing. She put one hand on the doorknob. The door swung slowly open. He could hear his own heart beating in his ears.

"It's kind of you to ask, but I don't think so, Mr. Butler."

Disappointment coursed through the big man. "Do you have other plans?"

"It isn't that. It's. . ." She seemed to be searching for a reason to refuse his invitation. "It makes extra work for Mac having so many to cook for. There's your daughter and son-in-law as well as all the hired help. Mac needs a day of rest."

"He doesn't mind. Mac loves to feed people. Besides, Carrie and Lucas won't be there this Sunday. They are having dinner with friends. Mac thinks highly of you, Miss Casey, and he's fond of Hope. He'd love to have you. We all would. Please reconsider. Say you will come."

Mariah rested her face against the top of Hope's dark head. "I don't know. . . ."

"Say yes, Mama." The small, dark head lifted from Mariah's shoulder. "I wanna see my kitten."

After a moment of stunned silence, both adults laughed, releasing the tension. "Hope and I will be pleased to accept your invitation, Mr. Butler."

He ruffled the little girl's dark curls. "Well then, I'll see you tomorrow."

"Good night, Mr. Butler."

"Good night, Miss Casey. Hope."

He stood looking at the closed door for a moment before turning away. Whistling softly to himself, he walked to his horse and swung into the saddle.

❧

Had Mr. Butler actually invited her to dinner? Mariah leaned against her closed front door until her heart resumed its normal rhythm. *"You are a fool, Mariah Casey."* Her mother's harsh voice spoke inside her head. *"Look at yourself, girl! Men like pretty women. Nobody wants a tall, gangly old maid."*

"Especially not a man like Sherman Butler." Sudden tears sprang to Mariah's eyes as she pushed away from the door and carried Hope to her bedroom. All those questions about whether or not she ever felt homesick. He probably thought she'd go running back to Ohio as soon as the school year ended. They hadn't been able to keep a teacher for longer than a year. Mr. Butler was only being nice to her so he wouldn't have to look for a replacement. She blinked back tears as she prepared Hope for bed.

By the time the little girl was in her nightgown Mariah was inwardly fuming. How dare that man think he could flatter her into staying in Cedar Bend. Well, she'd set him straight tomorrow after church. She would tell him Cedar Bend was her home, and she had no intention of going anywhere. He needn't waste his time wooing her. She had seen him talking to Emily James tonight. Let him court her.

She tucked Hope in and leaned over to kiss the little girl good night. Two little arms slipped around her neck. "I love you, Mama."

Another large chunk of the shell that encased Mariah's heart broke free and fell away. Mariah swept the little girl up into her arms. "Oh, Hope! I love you, too."

When a soft little kiss pressed against her cheek, Mariah burst into tears. A small hand patted her face. "Don't cry, Mama."

Knowing she mustn't frighten Hope, Mariah struggled to gain control of her emotions. "It's all right, honey. These are tears of joy."

The little girl snuggled closer. Mariah's heart twisted. She would gladly lay down her life for this child. She knew this was love. Pure, unmerited, *agape* love. For the first time she understood—at least as much as it was possible for a mortal to understand—the love that led Christ to the cross at Calvary.

Long after Hope was asleep, Mariah tossed and turned in her own bed. It had been the most emotionally exhausting day of her life. The sound of Hope's childish voice saying she loved her and the moist kiss the little girl had placed on her cheek moved her in a way she couldn't have imagined. Joy flooded her soul. No one had ever loved her before. *Thank You, Father, for bringing me to Cedar Bend. Thank You for bringing Hope into my life. Thank You for*— She felt herself drifting off to sleep, leaving her prayer unfinished. She knew God understood what was in her overflowing heart.

%

Sunday morning Mariah overslept. She knew she was going

to be late for Sunday school. Then, when Hope dawdled over breakfast, she realized they were going to be lucky if they made it in time for morning services. They were a block away when the church bell started tolling. When Hope refused to be hurried, she scooped her up into her arms and ran. At the foot of the steps she stood the child down and tried to catch her breath. There wasn't time. Still huffing and puffing like a steam engine, she clutched Hope's hand. Feeling decidedly frazzled—she hadn't even had time to do anything with her hair beyond twisting it into a loose roll and pinning it up in back—she rushed up the church steps. They stepped through the door as the bell pealed its final note. Sherman Butler was standing in the vestibule, talking to the pastor.

Even though he was facing them, for one frantic moment Mariah prayed he wouldn't see her. That somehow, miraculously, she would become invisible. Today was evidently not the day for miracles.

"Miss Casey." His blue eyes lit up and his dimples deepened. "I was beginning to think something had happened to you."

"No," she gasped and was too winded to say more.

Hope pulled away from Mariah and grabbed Mr. Butler's hand. "Mama slept and slept." She swung on his hand and smiled up at him. "We had to run all the ways to church."

He lifted one eyebrow, and if possible the dimples were even deeper. Mariah felt the color sweep up her neck to her hairline.

"Miss Casey," he began as he took her elbow with the hand Hope wasn't clinging to, "they are playing the opening hymn. May I escort you to your seat?"

"I—I—suppose so."

As soon as they stepped into the main sanctuary, Joanna, who was leading the singing, smiled. Every head turned.

Mariah shook off Sherman's hand. Head held high, she marched down the aisle a step ahead of him, past a gauntlet of faces. Some were smiling. Some, mostly the single women, were wearing a look of shocked disbelief. Thankfully Carrie Nolan was out of her line of vision.

She slid into the Jacobs's pew with a sigh of relief, leaving room for Hope to sit beside her. The little girl scrambled around Mariah and squeezed in between her and Gladys. Sherman, instead of continuing on to his accustomed seat, sat down in the space she had intended for Hope. It was a snug fit. Mariah was forced to scoot over as much as possible, but with the entire Jacobs family sitting on the other end of the pew, she couldn't move far. She lifted her chin. If Sherman Butler had set out to humiliate her, he was certainly succeeding.

They were barely seated when Joanna announced the next hymn and asked them to stand. Sherman took a hymnal from the rack on the back of the pew in front of them. Mariah never sang, but when he gestured for her to take one side of the book, she did. His arm brushed hers as they shared the hymnal, and her heart fluttered. *From all that running,* she assured herself. Though she had to admit, she did enjoy having him standing beside her. He was so big and tall that her eyes were barely level with his shoulder. Her hand, across the book from his large, callused hand, looked delicate. He wasn't much of a singer—a quality she found strangely appealing—though what he lacked in skill he made up for in enthusiasm. She found herself singing softly.

When Sherman went to the front to assist with the offering, Gladys leaned across Hope and whispered, "What happened last night after the dance?"

Mariah shook her head. "Nothing happened. He saw us home. That's all."

"Me an' Mama's gonna go home with Mistah Butlah afta church." Hope's voice was a notch above a whisper, and Mariah felt the color rushing to her face even as she shushed the little girl.

"No, we are not!"

"You pwomised I could see my kitty." Hope's lower lip shot out.

Mariah had never seen Hope cry, but she'd seen enough tantrums in her life to recognize when one was forthcoming. She couldn't deal with that today. "All right, we'll go," she whispered. "I promised her she could see her kitten," she explained to her cousin.

"I see." Gladys sat back in her seat with a satisfied smile.

"You do not see," Mariah hissed.

Her cousin turned to whisper to Lucille, who was leaning so far forward she was in danger of falling out of her seat. Mariah closed her eyes. She felt a headache coming on.

She expected Sherman to take his place with the rest of the Circle C crew after the offering. To her surprise he slid back into the pew beside her. She thought briefly of asking him to go sit with Cyrus and Mac, then decided that would only attract more attention. Besides, his daughter would rush to his rescue before the final "amen" was uttered. Until then she would just have to endure his presence. When the congregation stood to pray, the coarse fabric of his jacket brushed against her arm. She clutched the back of the seat in front of her with both hands and implored God to please help her make it through this day.

Don't let me like this man, Lord. Please. My life is so good right now. The prayer that began as a plea became a disjointed litany of praise. *Thank You, Father, for Hope. Thank You for giving me friends. Especially thank You for Joanna who accepts me the way I am. And for Dr. Brady, too. And, dear Lord, thank You for sweet, funny, wise, little Mac. Thank You for my family: Gladys, Lucille, and Nels.* Carrie Nolan's face flashed across her mind. She took a deep breath and added one final, oft-repeated plea. *Help me to like Carrie. And please, Lord, help Carrie to not dislike me so much. In Jesus' name. Amen.*

When they sat back down, Mariah put her arm around Hope. The little girl snuggled close. Resting her head against Mariah's side, she fell asleep. Mariah leaned back in the seat and felt the coarse fabric of Sherman's jacket sleeve across her shoulders. Jerking upright she turned to glare at him. He grinned at her and leaned close to whisper against her ear. "More room this way."

Mariah sighed, then still sitting stiffly erect so as not to touch his arm, turned her attention to Pastor Carson. It was difficult to focus on his message with Hope's little head burrowing into her side. Not to mention the man sitting beside her with his arm resting on the pew behind her. If she could only lay Hope down. She cast a quick glance down the pew. The Jacobs had room to scoot over several inches.

She touched Gladys's shoulder with her fingertip. When the woman turned to look at her, she motioned for them to move down. Her cousin glanced pointedly at Sherman's arm and smiled, then turned her attention back to the sermon. She endured five more minutes of discomfort before laying Hope over and cradling her head in her lap. A few minutes later her back began to spasm. She shifted, trying to find a more comfortable position, at the same time avoiding touching the muscular arm resting on the back of the seat. After she squirmed a second time she knew she had to do something. She glanced at Sherman. He appeared to be absorbed in the sermon. If she leaned back it wouldn't be as though he had his arm around her. He was only resting it there so they would have more room. She slowly allowed her body to relax against the back of the seat.

She looked at Sherman out of the corner of her eye. His attention was riveted on Pastor Carson. Mr. Butler was totally oblivious to her. She only wished that she could be so unaware of him.

After church Mariah was surrounded by a group of chattering women. To her relief they were more interested in Hope speaking than they were in Sherman Butler sitting beside her in church. At least that's what they talked about. Mariah heard the stories about their children and the various ages they began to talk and embarrassing things they said. Suddenly, Hope was no longer with her, and she had lost sight of Mac.

"I have to go," she said. "Mr. McDougal is waiting for us, and I have to find Hope."

The other ladies drifted away to their own families, but the town seamstress and her two friends refused to allow Mariah to leave.

"We heard you had been invited out to the Circle C for dinner," Mrs. Wright said with a forced smile.

"Yes, Hope wanted to go." Mariah thought she would nip any gossip about her and Sherman Butler in the bud. "She has a kitten out there she wants to see."

"Oh! So you have been there before?" The seamstress had the avid look of a hungry vulture on her thin face. Her friends were ready to pounce on Mariah when Mrs. Braun broke into their conversation.

"Hope is with L. K., dear." Hilda Braun linked her arm through Mariah's. "I am so happy she is finally speaking, but if she's like most children, there will be days you'll long for silence." She gently urged Mariah away from the three gossips. "Don't let them bother you," she said softly. "They're lonely and they chatter, but they have good hearts."

Mariah knew what it was to be lonely. If she hadn't come to Kansas and been given Hope, she might have become a gossip had she had anyone to gossip with. Back in Ohio, she had begun marking the date on the calendar when a couple married so she could count back from the date of their first child's birth. How despicable! She blushed at the memory.

"I know they mean well," she said. "But thank you for rescuing me."

"Mariah, it did my heart good to see Hope having such a good time last night. I had never seen her laugh before."

Mariah looked around the almost-empty room. "Where is Hope?"

"She's fine. She went outside with L. K., and Sherman and my Karl are with them. Mariah, Little Karl told me some time ago that Hope talked to him. I should have told you, but I didn't believe him."

Hope and L. K. had been inseparable since the first week of school. Mariah remembered all the times she'd seen the two children with their heads together. "I believe him," she said.

The two women stepped out into the chill October air. Mariah quickly scanned the almost-empty lot. Karl Braun and Sherman Butler stood talking beside the Brauns' large, two-seated surrey. The baby was in the front. Hope was in the backseat with the younger Braun children. The only other buggy was a sporty, dark blue phaeton she didn't recognize. Mac's black buggy was nowhere in sight, and neither was Sherman Butler's big bay gelding.

"Surely not," Mariah murmured.

"What is it, Mariah?"

"It's just that I thought—where is Mr. McDougal?"

"Mac has gone on home." Hilda Braun squeezed Mariah's arm. "Sherman told us you and Hope were going to have dinner at the Circle C."

"Yes, but I thought—when we went before, we rode out with Mac in his buggy. Mr. Butler always rides to church on that big red horse."

"Not today." Hilda laughed. "Don't worry, Mariah, you'll be fine. Mr. Butler is a gentleman, and you have a little chaperone."

Mariah's stomach was tied in knots as she allowed herself to be urged across the churchyard to where the two men were waiting. She felt so confused. What would she talk about on the trip out to the ranch?

thirteen

As it turned out, Mariah wasn't required to say much on the trip to the Circle C. Hope seemingly had stored up four years of questions against the day she would finally find her voice. And find it she had. Like water rushing over a broken dam, she asked questions. Lots of questions.

"How's come you only gots one horse, Mistah Butlah, an' L. K.'s daddy gots two?"

"Karl has a surrey. He needs two horses."

"Whatsa sarree?"

"It's like a big buggy."

"Oh." She took only a moment to digest this bit of information. "That's cause they gots lots of childruns."

"They have quite a few."

"Oh, look! See the jackrabbit, Hope?" Mariah felt as though her face was on fire.

"Wabbits has lots of babies, Mama. L. K. has a wabbit, and he says one day no babies, next day lotsa babies. Where you think all them baby wabbits comes from, Mama? Did God bring 'em?"

Mistah Butlah looked like he was about to explode. "Yes. I'm sure He did," Mariah answered.

Sherman snickered and Mariah glared at him. "Why don't you ask Mr. Butler? He's a rancher. He knows more about these things than I."

Hope looked up at the big man. He wasn't laughing now. "Mistah Butlah, how come the sky is blue?"

"Well, Hope—"

Mariah felt bad for putting Sherman on the spot and a little

116

embarrassed at Hope's questions. She tried to help the rattled rancher. "Oh, look over there! Wasn't that a deer, Hope?"

"I don't see no dee-ah."

"I think he's over there in the tall grass. If you'll be really still maybe you can see him."

"How do you know he's a him?"

"Shh! You'll frighten him."

Hope was relatively quiet after that—even shushing the adults when they tried to speak. Still, Mariah breathed a sigh of relief when they turned in the lane leading to the ranch house. She was thrilled that Hope was talking, but tomorrow she would teach her the word *discretion* and its definition.

Sherman reached his hand out to Mariah to assist her from the buggy. When her feet were firmly planted on the ground, he turned and held his hands up for Hope. The little girl was standing on the seat. Before Mariah could react, Hope launched herself into his arms.

"Hope!" Mariah gasped. "I told you that was dangerous and to never do it again. What if Mr. Butler had dropped you? You could be seriously injured."

"Mistah Butlah won't dwop me." Her little arms tightened around the big man's neck. "Will ya, Mistah Butlah?"

"Well, certainly not intentionally. But your mama is right. If my reaction time happened to be a hair off, I could miss you and you could get hurt."

"So promise me you won't do that again, Hope."

The lower lip shot out, but only momentarily. "Okay, Mama. Kin I see my kitty now?"

"After dinner."

"Okay, Mama."

When they stepped inside the kitchen, Mac was hobbling around, putting the finishing touches to dinner. "Jist hang yore wraps there." He indicated a long coat rack beside the kitchen door. "It's gittin' a mite nippy out there, ain't it?"

"I think I can feel snow in the air." Mariah unbuttoned Hope's coat and hung it up beside her shawl and bonnet. "What can I do to help?"

"I'd reckon you kin mash these here spuds." He handed Mariah a large, white apron and a potato masher.

"While you're doing that, I'll take care of the horse," Sherman said.

"Kin I go with Mistah Butlah to take keer of the horse? Please, Mama!"

Mariah looked down into the pleading eyes of the little girl clinging to her apron. She was so tiny. One of those huge beasts could step on her. "I'm afraid you would be in the way."

"Carrie spent a lot of time in the barn with me when she was small," Sherman said. "If you don't mind her going, I'll watch out for her."

"Please, Mama."

Mariah sighed. "All right. But I want you to pay very close attention to Mr. Butler and do what he tells you."

"I will, Mama."

Sherman helped Hope into her coat, and the two of them went out the door.

When they were gone, Mariah allowed herself to relax in Mac's friendly approval as she mashed potatoes and then made pan gravy.

"I ain't in the habit of sharin' my kitchen with jist anybody, Miss Casey. But I know yer a mighty good cook. You make the flakiest pie crust I ever et."

"I started cooking when I wasn't much older than Hope."

"I'll teach you to make red-eye gravy one-a these days," Mac promised. "An' one-a these days soon I'll learn ya how to make chili. I learnt the receipt when we was down in Texas."

"I've never seen chili. But I'd love to try it."

"Thet's good." Mac chuckled. "Sherm loves my chili. As I told you already, I tried to teach Carrie how to cook afore she got married, but she never could git the hang of it. 'Course her ma couldn't cook neither."

"Mrs. Butler couldn't cook?" Mariah had assumed there was nothing Caroline Butler hadn't been a master at.

"Not a lick." Mac was piling thick slices of baked ham on a platter. " 'Course Caroline was raised to be a lady. An' she was. Tweren't nobody better at visitin' the sick an' comfortin' the afflicted than Caroline Butler. Joanna Brady is like thet. Good-hearted an' lovin'. Thet's what Caroline was. Good-hearted. Ever'body loved her."

"I had envisioned Mrs. Butler as being perfect."

"Ain't nobody perfect, Mariah, 'cept one and thet's the Lord Jesus Christ." He placed the platter of ham in the center of the table. "Caroline was jist a flawed human bein' like the rest of us mortals. But she did reach out to the needy. And she did love the Lord with all her heart."

Mariah took the gravy and put it on the table beside the mashed potatoes. "Was she a good mother?"

"Course she was. She loved Carrie jist like you love yore little Hope." He put a gnarled hand on Mariah's arm. "I know yore ma failed you, Mariah, but thet ain't keepin' you from bein' a good ma to thet little girl. Iffen she didn't love you an' feel secure with you, she wouldn'ta started talkin'. I see the way yore face lights up when she calls you Mama."

Mariah felt tears brimming up in her eyes. "Mac, if only you knew. I used to dream of the day I would have a family to love. I gave up that dream a long time ago. Then to have Hope given to me. . . It's just—I can't even find the words. It's a miracle that, after all these years, God would entrust this beautiful child to my care."

"I reckon He couldn'ta give 'er to anyone more deservin'." Mac pulled a red bandanna from his hip pocket and blew his nose.

The door opened, and Hope burst into the room followed

by Sherman. "Mistah Butlah let me set on the horse."

"Hope, you have straw all over you. Here, let me pick it off. How on earth—"

"Mistah Butlah says I can wide. He says I'm a natchuwal— a natch—" She looked up at the man. "What did you say I was?"

"I said you were a natural horsewoman." He gave Mariah a sheepish smile. "Well, she is."

"I will not have my child on the back of some great beast."

"She wanted to sit on Tornado, and I didn't see any harm in it."

"Tornado! You put my little girl on the back of a horse named Tornado?"

"Her name's Tornado, but it's not what you think. She was born during a bad storm. She's gentle as a lamb. Besides, Hope wanted to."

Mariah was picking the last of the straw out of Hope's hair. "I suppose if she had wanted to jump out of the barn loft you would have let her." She looked from the straw between her fingertips to the man. Her eyes widened. "You didn't!"

"Carrie always liked to jump into the straw. There wasn't any way she could get hurt. Besides, she thought it was fun."

"*She* is a four-year-old who doesn't know the meaning of the word danger. You, on the other hand, are *supposed* to be a responsible adult."

Mariah rarely let her emotions get out of control. But the way Sherman Butler was standing there grinning at her made her furious.

"I'd reckon we'd better eat afore it gits cold," Mac said.

Cyrus had appeared from somewhere. She saw he was grinning, too. So was Mac. She took hold of Hope's wrist. "Come on, honey, and we'll wash your hands." She shot a scathing look at Sherman Butler. When she recognized that his amusement was directed at the situation, her irritation slipped away. No one was laughing at her. She straightened her shoulders and struggled to keep from smiling herself. "It's hard telling what *Mistah Butlah* let you get on your hands."

Mariah couldn't remember ever spending a more enjoyable afternoon. The two older men fussed over Hope, and she basked in their attention, while Sherman Butler engaged Mariah in conversation. Mariah forgot her shyness as she found herself sharing little anecdotes about her pupils back in Ohio. The big rancher hung on her every word as though what she had to say was important. When she told little stories that she found amusing, he laughed in all the proper places. She forgot that he was only being nice to her so he wouldn't have to look for another teacher in the fall. She even forgot that she wasn't pretty.

All too soon the meal ended. Mariah stood and began to help Mac clear the table. A gangly, teenaged boy Mac introduced as Andy Clark wandered into the kitchen. Mac took the stack of plates from Mariah's hands. "Andy'll do these dishes. This little lady wants to go see her kitten."

"She can wait until after the dishes are done."

"You an' Sherm take this here little gal to see thet kitten."

"Mama!" Hope's blue eyes pleaded. "You pwomised afta dinna I could see my kitty."

Sherman was buttoning Hope into her coat. "I feel guilty leaving you to clean up," Mariah protested, even as she draped her shawl around her shoulders.

"Pshaw!" Mac gave a dismissive wave of his hand. "You go on an' enjoy yoreself."

Mariah shivered as they followed Hope across the barnyard. Sherman stopped walking. "I'm going to run back to the house and get you a heavier wrap."

"I'm fine," Mariah insisted.

"I'm going to get a coat. I'll be back in a minute."

Before Mariah could protest further he was walking back

toward the house. Hope snuggled against her. "Mistah Butlah gonna take keer of you, Mama, just like you take keer of me."

Mariah put her arm around the little girl and drew her close. "Mr. Butler is a very thoughtful man."

"I likes Mistah Butlah."

Mariah watched the big man disappear into the house. She liked Mr. Butler, too. She only wished she didn't like him so much.

&

It was late afternoon when Sherman Butler's buggy passed beneath the arched entrance to the Circle C and turned onto the main road heading back to town. Mariah snuggled deeper into the folds of the coat that sheltered her from the biting wind. Hope, cocooned in the heavy blanket Mac had wrapped around her, slept with her head cradled in Mariah's lap.

"I wouldn't be surprised to see snow before morning," Sherman said.

"It's cold enough," Mariah agreed.

After a few more offhand remarks about the weather, a silence as warm and comfortable as the borrowed coat she wore enveloped the buggy. Mariah's thoughts turned to Hope and the kitten in the barn. The small ball of blind, yellow fluff had turned into a hissing bundle of wildness with razor-sharp claws and wouldn't let any of them near enough to touch it. Nevertheless, Hope insisted she was going to bring it home with her. When Mariah told her she couldn't have the kitten, letting her ride Tornado had narrowly averted a tantrum.

Mariah knew the black mare with the streaked blaze was smaller than the other horses. Still, she looked huge with Hope perched on her back. At least she had forgotten the kitten. Mariah sighed. Now she claimed Tornado.

She turned her gaze to the man driving the buggy. Today, when he wrapped his coat around her, his touch had been gentle. She had seen that same gentleness when he led the black horse around the corral. She felt safe with him. His big hands were steady on the lines, and his eyes never left the road. Sherman Butler was a good man. She wondered what he was thinking.

❧

Sherman's eyes were on the road, but his mind was elsewhere. He couldn't remember when he had spent a more enjoyable day. Hope had been on the verge of pitching a fit when Mariah told her she couldn't have the kitten. A smile tugged at his heart. She was a spunky little thing, considering how the Wainwrights had treated her.

Mariah was pretty spunky herself. He knew she had been nervous as a cat when he lifted Hope onto Tornado's back, but she'd kept her fears concealed from the child. Hope had taken to riding like a duck takes to water. He hadn't realized until today just how much he missed having a young one around.

He heard Mariah's soft sigh and glanced at her. She seemed lost in her own thoughts. He turned his eyes back toward the road. Today, when he came back from the barn, Mariah was bustling around the kitchen like she belonged there. Mac's kitchen was sacred ground. Except for his futile attempt to teach Carrie to cook, it was off-limits to outsiders. It had been all he could do to keep from laughing out loud. Then, when she started raking him over the coals for allowing Hope to jump out of the hayloft. . . Well, he had known for certain then. He wanted to spend the rest of his life with this woman.

❧

Mariah turned when Sherman cleared his throat. "I suppose you will be having Thanksgiving with your family."

She turned her head to look at him. "I hadn't really thought about it. Mother and I never did anything special for the holidays."

"Your mother is gone." Sherman's voice was gentle. "You will want to start your own traditions now that you have Hope."

Mariah looked down at the blanket-wrapped bundle resting between them. "I want Hope to have a happy childhood."

"She will have. You are doing a wonderful job with her, Miss Casey."

"Thank you, Mr. Butler." Mariah sighed. "Raising a child is much more difficult than I ever imagined it would be."

"Being responsible for another person's life is never easy. It was tough with Matthew and Carrie."

"Matthew? I thought Mrs. Nolan was an only child."

"My son died three months before Carrie was born. He was almost three years old."

"I'm so sorry." Mariah's heart ached for the man. "I didn't know."

"It was a difficult time. First, I lost my son. Then I lost my wife." He hesitated, searching for the right words. "I wanted Caroline to have everything she'd given up when she married me. I never realized until it was too late that those possessions meant nothing to my wife." Mariah felt his eyes on her. "You know the man in Luke that kept building bigger and bigger barns to store his goods? That was me, Miss Casey. I was angry after Caroline died. I know it was irrational, but I was angry at God for taking her, and I was angry at her for leaving. Then one day I realized, like the man in the Bible with his big barns and many possessions, if my soul were required of me I would have nothing to give."

Mariah wanted to say something comforting, but even if she found the words, she doubted she could force them past the lump in her throat.

"I was raised in a godly home. But I never knew Christ as my personal Savior until after Caroline was gone. Shortly after my wife died, I took a Bible and a jug of water and went to one of the line shacks. Stripped down to the basics, I read and prayed until I met my Lord. I want you to know I'm not the same angry man I was back then." He paused and took a deep breath before plunging on. "I wasn't a good husband to Caroline—how could I have been? We were unequally yoked. I cherished the things of this earth. Caroline's treasures awaited her in heaven. The only thing on this earth that mattered to Caroline was my salvation."

He brought the buggy to a halt in front of Mariah's house. Sitting in the buggy seat, he turned to face Mariah. "I'm not the same man I was then, Miss Casey. I wasn't the husband I should have been to Caroline, but I would be a good husband to you and a good father to Hope." He took a deep breath before continuing. "We haven't known each other long, but I know that I love you and I love Hope. Will you marry me, Mariah?"

Mariah sat in stunned silence. Had she heard Mr. Butler correctly? Had he said he loved her?

"I won't press you for an answer right now. Six months from now, after a proper courtship, I will ask you again. May I court you, Mariah?"

For the briefest moment her mother's sharp words about her undesirability echoed through Mariah's mind. She took a deep breath and forced them from her mind. "Yes, Mr. Butler. You may."

fourteen

That night after Hope was asleep, Mariah sat in the chair in her bedroom. Bible in hand, she mulled over the happenings of the afternoon. Had Mr. Butler truly said he loved her? He had asked her to marry him. She knew that. But love? Was it possible Mother had been wrong when she told her no man would ever love her? That she wasn't pretty enough?

She sighed and rested her head against the high back of the rocking chair. Mr. Butler was a fine-looking man. He was kind and gentle. Besides that, he had a huge ranch. She supposed he was wealthy, although she had never really thought about it. He could have any woman he wanted. What was it Carrie said that first Sunday she went to the ranch? *"Other women have set their caps for Papa, but he's never been interested in any of them."*

What of Carrie? Does she see me as a threat? Is that why she dislikes me so intensely? Could that be the reason for the lecture in front of her mother's portrait? She's already lost her mother. Is she afraid of losing her father, as well?

Mariah closed her eyes. After all these years, did she even want to marry? She had Hope. Wasn't that enough? True, she'd prayed for a husband. But did she really want one now? Husbands made demands. Her mother had certainly told her enough about that in the years after her father died. She could still hear her mother's voice. *"I thought if I married an old man I wouldn't have to be burdened with children."* Mother's laugh was harsh. *"You are proof that I was sadly mistaken."*

Sorrow overwhelmed Mariah. Her mother had possessed everything. She was beautiful. She was an accomplished homemaker. Before the accident, she had friends. If only she could have shown the least bit of affection their lives would have been so different. Mac said her mother was a foolish woman. And she had been. But more than that, she had been a woman trapped in the web of her own bitterness. What a waste!

As Mariah lifted her head and opened her eyes, the Bible slid to the floor. When she leaned over to pick it up she saw the corner of an envelope that had been hidden between the pages. She opened the Bible. Sherman Butler's letter. Had it been only two months since she received the offer of a position in Cedar Bend? She had been reading the twenty-ninth chapter of Jeremiah that day. As she looked down at the Bible, the eleventh verse reached out to her. She read the words of the Old Testament prophet aloud. " 'For I know the thoughts that I think toward you, saith the Lord, thoughts of peace, and not of evil. . . .' "

Mariah read the passage twice before leaning back in her chair. Had the last few months been ordered by God? Was it part of God's design for her life that she come to Kansas?

If I hadn't come to Cedar Bend, Hope wouldn't be sleeping in the other room now.

Was that why God had brought her here? To be Hope's mother? Was it also in His plan for her to be Sherman Butler's wife? But what of Carrie? She couldn't accept Mr. Butler's proposal without his daughter's approval. She had been praying for the young woman since the day after her arrival in Cedar Bend. She recalled some of the prayers. In retrospect those entreaties had contained a preponderance of the pronouns *I* and *me*. Had she really been praying for Carrie or had she been praying for herself?

The answer brought tears to Mariah's eyes. Except for the short plea this morning that she might come to like Carrie, most of her prayers had been centered on herself. Kneeling beside the chair in her bedroom, she asked God's forgiveness for her selfishness. Then she offered up the most heartfelt prayer of her life.

                                  ❧

Every Sunday morning, Sherman drove Mariah and Hope to church, then out to the Circle C for dinner. Mariah told no one but Joanna of his proposal.

Mariah and Hope spent Thanksgiving Day with the Jacobs. After a bountiful meal, the men gathered in the parlor with the children. The women retired to the kitchen to face a mountain of dirty dishes.

"Well, are you going to marry him or not?" Gladys asked.

Mariah dropped a dish towel on the floor and bumped her head on the kitchen table when she bent to retrieve it. "About whom are you speaking, Cousin Gladys?"

"You know very well who I am talking about, young lady." The older woman held a damp cloth against the red spot on Mariah's forehead. "Sherman Butler, that's who."

Gladys's daughters were watching with wide-eyed interest. Mariah realized she was blushing. "Mr. Butler is a good friend."

"Good friend, indeed!" her cousin scoffed.

"Mr. Butler brings Mariah and Hope to church every Sunday morning," Lucille told Clara, her out-of-town sister. "He sits beside her, and"—Lucille paused, seemingly for drama's sake—"he even puts his arm around her. It is so romantic!"

"Is Mr. Butler courting you, Cousin Mariah?" Clara asked.

"Of course he is." Gladys removed the cloth from Mariah's forehead. "If you could see them together you wouldn't have to ask."

"Oh, Cousin Mariah!" Clara threw her arms around her cousin. "I am so happy for both of you!"

Mariah returned her cousin's brief embrace before turning back to the dishpan.

"So have you accepted him yet?" Gladys persisted.

"I don't recall saying that he'd asked." Mariah slid a plate into the steaming rinse water.

"If he hasn't, he soon will." Gladys dried the plate and handed it to Lucille. "So you are going to accept him, aren't you?"

Mariah plunged her hands into the soapy water. "I don't know," she said honestly.

"Why ever not?" Clara asked. "Mr. Butler is quite a catch."

This was her family, and she knew they cared about her. Mariah took a deep breath. "Well, for one thing, there's his daughter. She doesn't like me."

"Carrie?" Lucille gave a dismissive wave of her slender hand. "I wouldn't worry about her."

"There are other considerations." Mariah rubbed at an invisible spot on the plate she was washing.

"Here." Gladys took the plate from her hands. "Let me have that before you rub a hole in it."

Mariah saw two little splashes in the dishwater. Lifting a soapy hand she swiped at her tears.

Gladys put her arm around her. "Sometimes a good cry puts things in perspective. Isn't that right, girls?" She led Mariah to a chair and urged her to sit down.

Through a blur of tears Mariah saw the concern on their faces. Not avid interest, like the three gossips at church, but genuine, loving concern.

She buried her face in the clean tea towel Clara pressed into her hand and released a lifetime of pain. While gentle hands caressed her back and shoulders, the last segment of the shell that had imprisoned her heart for so many years shattered and fell away. She wiped her face and blew her nose on the towel.

"Well, I guess we had better not dry dishes on that," she said.

They all laughed. Then Gladys pulled up a chair, facing Mariah. "Now, why don't you tell us what is really bothering you?"

Lucille and Clara pulled up their own chairs between Gladys

and Mariah, forming a circle. They looked at her expectantly.

"First of all, I want to tell all three of you how much I love you. Secondly, I want you to promise you won't breathe a word of what I'm about to say to anyone."

"We will respect your confidence, dear," Gladys promised. "You should know that."

"Our lips are sealed," Clara said, while Lucille raised her hand to her mouth and pantomimed a key turning in a lock.

Mariah breathed a shaky sigh as she wadded the soggy dish towel in trembling hands. "Mr. Butler did ask me to marry him."

"I knew it," Gladys exulted. "I just knew it."

"Will the wedding be after school dismisses for the summer?" Clara asked.

"I don't know if there will be a wedding." Mariah twisted the dish towel. "I don't know if I can marry Mr. Butler."

"Why not?" Clara leaned forward. "Cousin Mariah, do you have any idea how many women have tried to snag Sherman Butler? Even I, before I met George, cast a speculative eye in his direction."

"Half the women in Cedar Bend have," Lucille said. "The other half are already married."

"Sherman Butler has never lacked opportunities," Gladys said. "But, until you came to town, I never knew him to give any woman a second glance."

"It's plain to see he is smitten by you," Lucille interjected. "The unmarried women of Cedar Bend are so jealous."

Clara put a hand on Mariah's arm. "You do love him, don't you, Cousin Mariah?"

"I don't know." Mariah pleated the dish towel between her fingers. "Until I came to Kansas I didn't know what love was. I admire Mr. Butler greatly, but love. . . I don't know."

"Surely you want a husband and children of your own," Clara said.

"I thought I did at one time. When I was younger I prayed for that very thing, but now—" Mariah looked down as her hands worried the dish towel. "God has given me Hope. It seems greedy to want more. Besides, there's the problem of Carrie. I will not come between Mr. Butler and his daughter."

Gladys took Mariah's hand in hers. "Carrie will come to love you once she knows you."

"She might," Mariah agreed, although her voice was laced with doubt. "But that's not my only concern." With her free hand she wiped a fresh tear from her face.

"Mariah, dear," Gladys said as she squeezed the younger woman's hand, "are you worried about the more intimate aspects of marriage?"

Mariah looked down at the dish towel in her lap. "Mother said it was horrible."

"Mariah, look at me!" Gladys put her fingertips under the younger woman's chin and lifted her head until their eyes met. "Mariah, your mother was wrong. The first marriage was performed by God in the Garden of Eden. Our heavenly Father decreed we were to be one with our husbands. This is not a curse, child. It's a blessing. A gift from God. Didn't Jesus say the Father gives His children good gifts? I know it is not proper to speak ill of the dead, but Margaret found no joy in anything but her own reflection in the mirror. I can only imagine what your life was like with that woman after she believed her beauty was gone." She pulled Mariah into a loving embrace. "You have nothing to fear from Sherman Butler, dear. He is a kind, gentle man. He would never do anything to hurt you."

"Mr. Butler is a handsome man. He deserves a pretty wife," Mariah murmured against Gladys's shoulder.

Gladys put her hands on Mariah's shoulders and pushed her away so she could look into her eyes. "You're beautiful, Mariah. I've noticed the way Sherman Butler's face lights up when he looks at you. I'd dare say in Mr. Butler's eyes you are *very* beautiful. As for Carrie—" She released Mariah and stood. "Well, we will all pray for her, and she'll come around. Now, girls, let's finish these dishes."

❧

When the kitchen was finally in order, the women joined the men in the parlor. Clara's two children and Hope napped in Lucille's old room. Outside, the shadows were beginning to lengthen. Mariah sat on the sofa with Lucille's three-month-old son lying lengthwise on her lap.

"You're such a pretty boy," she cooed. He responded with a bubbly grin that made Mariah wish she could have held Hope when she was this age.

"Take his hands and pull him up," Lucille said.

"Don't I need to watch his head?"

"He can already hold his head up," Lucille said with maternal pride. "He's very advanced for his age."

"Of course he is." Mariah looked down at the baby in her lap. She imagined his fine, black hair as copper curls. Her face grew warm at where her thoughts were leading.

"I think we have company." Nels struggled out of his chair.

"I didn't hear anyone knock," Clara's husband, George, said.

"Daddy always sits where he can look out the window," Clara explained. "He must have seen someone coming."

Mariah heard the outside door leading from the porch into the front hallway open and close, but she was too involved with the baby to look up.

❧

Nels opened the door before Sherman had a chance to knock. "Is Miss Casey still here?"

"She is." Nels swung the door wide. "Come on in out of the cold, Sherm. Let me take your coat and hat."

While Nels took care of his outer garments, Sherman sat down on a bench and pulled off his boots.

"The family is in the parlor."

Sherman stepped through the door behind Nels. He returned the Jacobs family's greetings, but his attention was on Mariah. She looked up and her eyes widened. "Mr. Butler, whatever are you doing here?"

"I thought I would come in and drive you and Hope home." He crossed the room and sat down on the sofa beside her. "This little fellow is growing like a weed, Lucille."

The young mother beamed. "You can hold him if you like, Mr. Butler."

"It's been a long time." Sherman took the baby from Mariah and lifted him to his shoulder. "But I reckon I need the practice for the day Carrie makes me a grandpa."

"Who knows?" Jed teased. "You might have one of your own before then."

Sherman looked at Mariah. She was mighty fetching in a sapphire blue dress that matched her eyes. "I just might."

Mariah's face flushed bright crimson. At the same time, Sherman felt a gush of warmth on his shoulder. Lucille sprang up, her face almost as red as her cousin's. "I'm so sorry, Mr. Butler." She grabbed her son.

Gladys appeared with a damp cloth, fretting at the milk stain despite Sherman's protests. Mariah put a hand over her mouth, her blue eyes danced, and her shoulders shook with merriment. It was worth smelling like sour milk if it made her laugh.

❧

That night, lying in her bed, Mariah's thoughts were on the events of the day. Her heart had caught in her throat when she saw Sherman standing in his stocking feet behind Cousin Nels. She hadn't been the only one who was happy to see him. When Hope woke from her nap, she ran straight to Sherman and climbed on his lap.

Today in the kitchen with Cousin Gladys and her girls, I felt I truly belonged to a family for the first time. Sitting beside Sherman and Hope on the sofa, I felt complete. I do love him, Lord. Beyond any shadow of a doubt. If Carrie could accept me, I would marry him tomorrow.

fifteen

The week after Thanksgiving brought a foot of snow. On Monday morning, Mariah slogged through the drifts, pulling Hope on the sled Sherman had given her. Her thoughts were on the Christmas program. Some of the parts were going to be easy to cast. Mabel Carson with her dark hair and eyes would be perfect as Mary. Jay Braun would be Joseph. The angels and shepherds would be no problem. But what could Mark Hopkins do? The young man stood head and shoulders above her other pupils. In three months he had advanced to the fifth reader. She wouldn't leave him out for the world.

Mariah sighed. Joanna had offered to help her with the music and costumes. Perhaps she could come up with something.

"Mark will be perfect as the angel Gabriel," Joanna said, when Mariah broached the subject to her that evening.

"Of course!" Mariah exclaimed. "Why didn't I think of that?"

Joanna laughed. "Two heads are better than one. What are you going to do with the little ones?"

"Do you think anyone will be offended if they are sheep?"

"Why should they be?" Joanna asked. "After all, what is a shepherd without sheep?"

The next morning Mariah assigned parts. Since Pastor Carson would read the Christmas story from the book of Luke, there were few lines to memorize. That afternoon, she and Joanna began to transform the cast-off clothing they had collected into costumes. They only had a week until the first rehearsal.

❧

"Everything is coming together beautifully," Mariah told Sherman the following Sunday as they rode back to town from the Circle C.

"Me an' L. K. is sheeps," Hope volunteered from her place between them on the seat of the open sleigh. "Mama made us sheeps hats out of a blanket."

Sherman smiled down at the little girl. "You look more like a little lamb to me. What do you want Saint Nick to bring you for Christmas, my little lamb?"

Hope giggled; then her small face turned serious. "I wants a daddy. Mistah Butlah, will you be my daddy?"

Sherman looked at Mariah. "I reckon you'll have to talk to your mama about that."

Mariah turned her head away, but not before Sherman saw the sheen of tears in her blue eyes. "What about it, Mama?" he asked gently. "This little lamb wants a daddy."

"You promised me six months," she said, with her face still averted.

"And I will honor that promise." There wasn't much more he could say in Hope's presence. Sherman shrugged his shoulders and turned his attention back to the snow-packed road.

❧

The program was held at the Community Church the Sunday evening before Christmas. Joanna peeked around the makeshift curtains she and Mariah had hung to separate the stage from the rest of the building.

"The room is filled to overflowing," she whispered.

As soon as the children were in their places for the first scene, Mariah and Joanna sat down on the front pew. A visiting minister offered a lengthy prayer. Then Pastor Carson began to read. " 'And it came to pass in those days, that there went out a decree from Caesar Augustus, that all the world should be taxed. . . .' "

When he read the final verses in the passage, two of the older boys pulled the curtains aside to reveal Mary and Joseph kneeling behind the straw-filled manger. Joanna stood to lead the congregation in singing "Away in a Manger."

The curtains closed at the end of the song. While Pastor Carson resumed reading, Mariah and Joanna slipped behind the curtain to arrange the next scene.

" 'And there were in the same country shepherds abiding in the field, keeping watch over their flock by night.' "

The curtains slid open to reveal shepherds and sheep while Joanna led "The First Noel." The little sheep were a bit fidgety. Hope kept looking around and waving to people in the audience. Mariah couldn't suppress a smile. At least the *friendly* sheep wasn't talking.

Soon the curtain closed for the final time. After the congregation sang the final Christmas hymn, the minister gave another prayer in conclusion. Then Mariah and Joanna stepped forward to thank everyone who had come. Joanna slipped away as parents surrounded Mariah, congratulating her on the program and voicing appreciation for her teaching.

*

Sherman watched Mariah accept the accolades she deserved. She was wearing a cranberry-colored dress he had never seen before. Dark curls framed her flushed face. Her blue eyes glowed as she talked to her students and their parents.

"Isn't she beautiful?" he murmured to Carrie, who was standing beside him.

"Who? Miss Casey?" Carrie shrugged her shoulders. "Getting rid of those drab clothes and that horrible bun improved her looks, I suppose. But I wouldn't describe her as beautiful. My mama was beautiful."

"I wish you would go up and say a few words to her, Carrie. You haven't been able to come to Sunday dinner for several weeks now." He patted her shoulder. "You don't want Mariah to think you are avoiding her."

"Mistah Butlah!" Hope pushed past several people to tug on his hand. "Did you see me? I was the sheep that waved at you."

"I certainly did, my little lamb." Sherman picked the little girl up. "You were the best one up there."

Hope wrapped one arm around his neck. "I waved to you, too, Miss Carrie. Did you see me?"

"I saw you. You made an excellent sheep."

"Well, my little lamb, would you like to help me pass out treats?"

Lucas put his arm around Carrie's shoulders. "Come on, darlin', let's go tell Miss Casey how much we enjoyed the program. And you, little miss," he said, squeezing Hope's hand, "have fun helping Mr. Butler pass out treats."

"I will." Hope leaned out of Sherman's arms to plant a moist kiss on Carrie's cheek. "Bye, Miss Carrie. Bye, Mistah Lucas."

❧

"Your son is a delight to have in the classroom," Mariah told Mark Hopkins's parents. "If he continues to advance at this rate, he will graduate in April."

"Mark's a good boy," Mr. Hopkins replied. "I just want to thank you for all the time you've devoted to him, Miss Casey."

"I'm very fond of Mark, Mr. Hopkins. As I said before, he's a delight to work with."

After the Hopkins moved on, Mariah turned and came face-to-face with Carrie Nolan and her husband, Lucas.

"I thought you didn't get involved with your pupils, Miss Casey," Carrie offered without preamble.

"Good evening, Mrs. Nolan. Mr. Nolan." Mariah briefly rested her hand on the younger woman's arm. "I want to apologize to you for what I said that day. It was rude and entirely uncalled for."

"We wanted to tell you how much we enjoyed the program," Lucas said.

"Thank you, Mr. Nolan." Mariah smiled. "But I can't accept all the credit for that. I couldn't have done it without Joanna's help."

"Mac told me you and Hope will be spending Christmas Day at the Circle C."

"We were invited," Mariah said. "You will be there, won't you?"

"The Circle C is my home, Miss Casey. Nothing, and nobody, will keep me from celebrating Christmas with my family."

Mariah longed to put her arms around the younger woman. This was neither the time nor place. She smiled and told them she was looking forward to seeing them Christmas Day.

☙

As Sherman drove Mariah and Hope home after the program, the still-excited girl chattered about the program. "I was the bestest sheep," she said. "Mistah Butlah sayed so. So's did Uncah Mac an' Uncah Cy'us. Evahbody sayed I was."

"I think I'm going to have to teach someone the meaning of the word H-U-M-I-L-I-T-Y," Mariah said.

"I hope you have better luck than you did with D-I-S-C-R-E-T-I-O-N." Sherman laughed.

"Mama, you know what I gots in my sack?" Hope clutched the treat bag to her. "I gots an apple an' some peppahmint sticks an' a o'ange thing. What is that o'ange thing, Mama?"

"The orange thing is an orange, Hope." Mariah hugged her close. "Mr. Butler had them shipped all the way from Florida."

Before Mariah could stop her, Hope took a bite of the orange. She made a face and spit the piece of peeling out. "I don't like o'anges," she said.

"It's supposed to be peeled," Mariah explained. "When we

get home, I'll peel it for you. Then I think you will like it."

Hope returned the orange to the sack and folded the top down. "I'll eat my apple, Mama. You kin have the ol' o'ange."

Sherman chuckled, then said, "You did a good job on the program, Mariah. I was proud of you."

"Thank you, Mr. Butler." She strained to see his face in the dim glow of the sleigh's lanterns. "I couldn't have done it without Joanna."

"Didn't I see Joanna with your star pupil after the program?"

"Mark escorted Joanna home," Mariah said. "He's exhausted the library at school. Joanna has been loaning him books."

"I thought they might be keeping company."

"No," Mariah said. "Mark and Joanna are friends. That's all."

"Ma'k's sweet on Aunt Joanna," Hope interrupted. "Julie telled me so."

Julie was Mark Hopkins's six-year-old sister and a prominent member of Hope's growing circle of friends.

"I believe Julie is mistaken," Mariah said. "Mark and Joanna have been friends for years. Nothing more."

"From what I've seen, Hope and Julie are right," Sherman said. "That young man's got that certain glow in his eyes when he looks at Joanna. The same glow I get when I look at you, Miss Casey."

A pleasurable warmth enveloped Mariah. "What a thing to say, Mr. Butler," she scolded. "Especially in front of the C-H-I-L-D."

"I's not a child, Mama," Hope said. "I's a girl."

Sherman chuckled. "How well can she spell, Miss Casey?"

"Obviously better than I thought she could." Mariah laughed. "I knew she was learning to read, of course. And I knew she loved books, but I thought she mostly looked at the pictures."

When Sherman walked them to the door, he bent down and whispered in Mariah's ear. "I love you, Mariah."

Mariah stood in the open doorway with Hope at her side and watched through swirling snowflakes as he climbed into the sleigh. She could still feel his warm breath on her ear. *I love you, too, Sherman Butler.*

She didn't go inside and close the door until the sleigh and its driver were swallowed up by darkness.

❧

On Christmas Eve, Mariah and Hope had dinner with the Jacobs. As they exchanged gifts, Mariah looked around the parlor at her family: Nels, Gladys, Jed, and Lucille with baby Lawrence. She then hugged Hope, who was snuggled on her lap. She felt a sense of belonging she had never experienced before coming to Kansas. This was her family. She loved every one of them. And she felt secure in their love for her.

Later, after Jed had driven Mariah and Hope home, she sat on the edge of Hope's bed and read Clement Moore's poem, " 'Twas the Night Before Christmas," to her. After she closed the cover of the book, the questions began. What was a kerchief? What was a sugarplum? What? Why? Where? When? How?

When Hope ran out of questions, Mariah said her prayers with her then kissed her good night. After the little girl's eyes closed, Mariah went into her own bedroom. She took from the wardrobe the doll she had made for Hope. It wasn't pretty like the china dolls at the mercantile, but it was soft and durable, and every stitch was sewn with love. A little girl could hug this doll and sleep with it and feed it strawberry jam and love it without fear of it breaking. Mariah smoothed the flannel gown that was fashioned from leftover scraps of Hope's gown. There were three outfits made of scraps from Hope's dresses still hidden in the wardrobe. Tomorrow she would give them to her.

Mariah lifted the covers and slipped the doll in beside the sleeping child. Hope, who slept like a rock, never stirred.

Mariah kissed one of her rosy cheeks and tucked the quilts around her. Hope would be so surprised when she woke tomorrow and found the doll. Mariah smiled and went to her own bed.

ঌ

"Mama! Mama! Look what I gots." The excited little girl stood beside Mariah's bed, clutching the doll. "Did Saint Nick bwing her, Mama?"

Mariah lifted the covers. "Climb in with me before you freeze."

Hope snuggled next to Mariah under the covers. "Where did her come fwom, Mama?"

"Do you like her, Hope?" Mariah waited while Hope examined the doll's embroidered face and stroked her dark brown yarn hair.

"I love her, Mama." She hugged the doll close. "Did Saint Nick bwing her? Or did God bwing her?"

"What do you think?" Mariah hugged Hope as tightly as she was hugging her new doll.

Hope's small face twisted in concentration as she mulled the question. "Mrs. Harris say every good an' perfect gift comes fwom God." Her expression relaxed. "Saint Nick isn't weal, Mama. The story you wed to me is make-believe. Weinde-ahs can't weally fly. God is weal, Mama. He gived me you. An' He gived me my dolly."

Mariah blinked back tears as she kissed Hope's smooth forehead. "However did you get so smart in only four years, honey?"

Hope giggled. "You teached me."

Mariah gave the little girl a final squeeze. "You stay here with your baby while I build up the fire."

Mariah slipped from the bed, slid her feet into cold slippers, threw on a robe, and ran across the icy floor. While she waited for the kitchen to warm up, she looked out the frosty kitchen window. Last night's snow had added six inches to what was already on the ground. A few snowflakes still hung in the frigid air. In the east the sun was rising, dispelling the few clouds that remained. It was going to be a beautiful day.

sixteen

Mariah bustled around the kitchen helping Mac put the finishing touches on dinner. The roaring fire in the fireplace combined with the heat from the big, black range warmed the large room. Mariah felt comfortable in Mac's presence. As she had from their first meeting, she shared her deepest feelings with him.

"Before last night at Cousin Gladys's I never celebrated a family Christmas," Mariah said. "There was something so special about gathering with family to share a meal and exchange gifts." She touched the brooch pinned in the froth of white lace at the throat of her cranberry red dress. "Joanna gave me this. It is my first Christmas gift. Actually, I believe it is my first gift ever. Not that the gifts are the important thing," she hastened to explain. "What makes it special is the love we share. Before I came to Kansas I didn't know what—" Her voice broke off as she turned and saw Carrie standing in the doorway.

How long had she been there? How much had she overheard? Mariah set the dish of sweet potatoes on the table. "Mrs. Nolan, is Hope all right?"

"Hope is fine. Lucas and Papa are entertaining her." She stepped into the kitchen. "Mac, is there anything I can do to help?"

Mac raised a bushy eyebrow. "I reckon you kin set the table in the dining room, little lady. Then you kin help us git the grub on the table."

"All right. I can do that." Carrie started to leave, then turned back. "Where are the dishes you want me to use?"

"Caroline Abigail Butler, you lived in this house fer nineteen years. You know as well as I do thet the good chiner's in the sideboard."

"Oh! That's right!" Carrie turned on her heel and left.

"Thet girl's as useless around the kitchen as her ma wuz," Mac grumbled. "Course Caroline had an excuse. She wuz raised to be a lady. Her pa had folks hired to wait on her hand and foot. She never had to lift a finger to do nothin' afore she married Sherman. The little lady is different. Carrie was born right here. I tried to learn her, but I don't know—" The old man shook his head. "Mebbe bein' a lady is jist bred into her. You know my ma always said you cain't beat out of the bones what's born in the blood."

Mariah moved to the stove. "You have all done a fine job raising her," she said. "Mrs. Nolan is a secure young woman, and she certainly has many talents." Mariah stirred the gravy. "She's as comfortable on horseback as most people are in a rocking chair."

"Carrie kin ride all right." Mac deftly transferred the roasted goose from pan to platter. "You oughta see her at the roundup."

Mac cast a speculative look in Mariah's direction. "I jist had me an idee. Why don't you come with us on the spring roundup?"

"Oh, my! I couldn't do that." Mariah poured the gravy into a large gravy boat. "I have school. Then there's Hope. Besides, horses make me nervous and cows frighten me. What would I do on a roundup?"

"Help me with the cookin'." Mac put a gnarled hand to the small of his back. "My rheumatiz is actin' up. You know I ain't as young as I once was, an' feedin' thet crew is a lot of work. I sure could use yore help, Mariah."

"I would like to help, Mac. But there's school and—"

"School will be out jist afore roundup," Mac said. "And

Hope kin come right along with you. The two of you kin ride out with me in the chuck wagon. You kin sleep in the wagon, too. Carrie done it ever since she weren't no bigger than Hope."

"I don't know, Mac. It would be an adventure. But there are other considerations besides school and Hope."

"You think on it, Mariah. You got plenty of time to decide. It ain't 'til April."

Mariah promised Mac she would let him know as soon as she arrived at a decision. Then Carrie came back to the kitchen, and she didn't think about the roundup again that day.

Later, gathered in the living room in front of a blazing fire, Mariah gave Carrie and each of the men a small, beautifully wrapped package. The four men immediately ripped the paper from their gifts.

Sherman, Lucas, and Cyrus were so lavish in their praise of the woolen socks that Mariah blushed. Only Mac remained silent. He examined the heavy brown socks for so long Mariah was afraid he didn't like them. She was on the verge of apologizing for her poor choice of gifts when he cleared his throat and looked up.

"Well, would you looka here! Wool socks. Did you knit these yerself, Mariah?"

Mariah nodded. "It's a small token of my affection."

"I ain't had a pair of hand-knitted socks since the war." Mac pulled a red bandanna from his hip pocket and blew his nose. "My Emily knit socks fer me afore I went away."

A wave of remorse swept over Mariah. Without thinking, she rose from the couch where she was sitting with Hope and Sherman. Two steps and she dropped to her knees beside Mac's chair. "I'm sorry. It wasn't my intention to bring back sad memories. I recall Mrs. Dodd—she was one of the older members of Father's flock—talking about sending her husband wool socks when he was in the war. I should have known your wife knit socks for you." Mariah put her arms around the old man she had come to regard as a dear friend. "Please forgive my foolishness."

"My memories of Emily an' my little boy ain't sad ones, Mariah. You know thet. I'm mighty proud of these socks." Mac patted the arm that encircled him. "Now you go back an' set with Sherman an' yer little girl."

Mariah had an urge to kiss Mac's bristly cheek, but she wasn't quite brave enough, so she gave him a hug and returned to the couch. Sherman's big hand squeezed her shoulder. Mariah looked over Hope's head and into his clear, blue eyes. He had told her twice that he loved her, but the tenderness reflected in his eyes spoke more eloquently of the depth of his feelings than words ever could. With all the strength she could muster, Mariah turned her head.

Seated on the couch across from them beside Lucas, Carrie was staring at her. Mariah would have expected to see hatred, or even the usual disdain on the young woman's face. What she saw was pain so deep it tore at her heart. The young woman's gaze moved to her father, and the expression deepened to heart-wrenching agony.

"Aren't you goin' to open your gift, Caroline?" Carrie had put the small package aside when Mariah handed it to her. When she showed no indication that she intended to unwrap it, Lucas nudged her gently with his elbow. "Come on, darlin', let's see what Miss Casey gave you."

For a heartbeat Mariah thought the younger girl was going to refuse. Then, her movements lackadaisical, Carrie removed the wrapping and looked down at the delicately embroidered, hem-stitched set of linen collar and cuffs. Tears welled up in her eyes. "Please! I need a drink of water. Don't wait for me."

She handed the package to her husband and fled the room.

"I'd reckon I'd better go see about her," Lucas said.

"No, I'll go." Sherman patted Mariah's shoulder. "We won't be long."

❧

Sherman found Carrie sitting at the kitchen table, her head down, a full glass of water in front of her. "Caroline Abigail, you owe Miss Casey an apology," he said without preamble. "I want you to march right back in there and thank her, and I want you to apologize for your rudeness."

"How could you, Papa?" Carrie raised a tearstained face to him. "I saw the way you looked at that woman. How could you do that to Mama?"

Confronted with the evidence of her misery, Sherman's anger fled. "I'm not doing anything to your mama, little girl." He pulled out a chair and sat down beside her. "I love Mariah, Carrie."

"You told me no one would ever take Mama's place." Carrie's tear-filled brown eyes accused him. "You lied to me, Papa."

"I didn't lie to you, little girl. Mariah isn't taking your mama's place; she has a place of her own." Sherman placed his hand over Carrie's clenched fist. "I have asked Mariah to be my wife."

Carrie pulled her hand from under his. A sob tore from her throat. "How do you think Mama would feel knowing you were marrying another woman?"

"Your mother would be happy for me. It's your behavior that would shame her." Suddenly Sherman saw what had been right in front of him all the time. The reason Mariah wouldn't marry him was sitting at the table beside him. He sprang to his feet and loomed over the child he cherished more than his own life.

"I know you and Mariah got off on the wrong foot, but you have never given her a chance. You have been rude and hateful to her from the beginning."

"*I've* been rude!" Carrie's temper flared. "I told you how she behaved that day at school. Demanding a key, telling me the room was improperly organized, saying she didn't get involved with her students. Besides that she jumped all over me because I was late."

"Well, you were late," Sherman retorted. "As for the key, Mariah didn't come from a small place like Cedar Bend where people can be trusted. And she is an experienced teacher, Carrie. She knows how a classroom should be arranged. I have no idea why she said she didn't get involved with her pupils. She spends hours working with the children. She is fond of them, and they all seem to love her. You know that."

"She's pretending to be different." Carrie pushed her chair back and stood to face her father. "And now I know why."

"What exactly is that supposed to mean?"

"She's just trying to snag you. I'll bet she couldn't say yes fast enough when you asked her to marry you."

All the anger drained out of Sherman as quickly as it had come. "She didn't say yes, Carrie."

The astonished expression on Carrie's face would have been amusing if the circumstances had been different. "She didn't say anything. I promised her time to think about it."

"Why wouldn't she say yes?" Carrie frowned. "There must be a reason."

"Yes, there must be," Sherman agreed. "Why don't you think about it, little girl, and see if you can figure out why Mariah would reject my proposal?" He put an arm around her and drew her close. "Honey, all I ask is that you give Mariah a chance. All right?"

"All right." Carrie buried her face against his shirt. "I will for you, Papa."

Sherman pushed her gently from him. "Wash your face, and as soon as you feel able come back to the living room."

He turned at the door. "And, Carrie, it would be nice if you thanked Mariah for the gift."

❧

Mariah looked up from where she was sitting on the couch with Sherman and Hope when Carrie rejoined them. Sitting down beside Lucas, Carrie picked up the discarded gift. After carefully examining the delicate embroidery and neat hemstitching, she lifted her head, and her gaze shifted from her father to Mariah.

"Thank you, Miss Casey." Her eyes were swollen and red, her voice little more than a whisper. "You must have spent hours on these."

"You are welcome, Carrie." Mariah's heart ached for the young woman. "I enjoyed making them for you."

That evening, on the way home, Mariah and Hope nestled under a buffalo skin robe. With the moon reflecting off the thick blanket of snow it was as light as midafternoon. The first mile or so Hope chattered about her gifts, then clutching the rag doll Mariah made for her—the doll she had named Jake for some inexplicable reason—she fell asleep. Silence as deep as the night that surrounded them enveloped the sleigh.

Mariah didn't object when Sherman carried Hope into her bedroom and laid her on her bed. While he went outside to finish unloading the sleigh, Mariah pulled the covers snugly around the little girl and the doll she refused to relinquish even in sleep. After she kissed Hope good night and whispered a prayer over her, Mariah, still wearing her coat, went into the parlor. Sherman was building a fire in the parlor stove.

She watched him close the stove door and adjust the damper. He had never been in her home before. She saw the room as she imagined he must see it. The needlepoint, the crocheted antimacassars and doilies, the hooked rugs. All the fussy, meaningless froufrou she had created on thousands of empty evenings. And she saw how he filled her parlor with his presence.

⁊

Mariah's house was pretty much as Sherman had imagined it. Spotlessly clean and feminine, but homey. Hope's books were scattered about. A small stocking was draped over the arm of a chair. A large, black Bible lay open on a chair-side table. He turned away from the stove. Mariah was standing in the doorway. The soft lamplight shadowed her face, but her luminous blue eyes spoke to him.

He cleared his throat. "I've got your fire going."

Her gaze shifted, then came back to rest on his face. "Thank you."

"I put Hope's things over there." He gestured to the corner. "I wasn't sure where you would want them."

"That's fine." Mariah looked at the small rocking chair, the wire-wheeled wagon, and an assortment of smaller gifts. "Everyone was so generous. I know this is a Christmas Hope will never forget." A slight smile touched the corners of her mouth. "Don't you think the horse was a bit extravagant, Mr. Butler?"

"Nope." Sherman chuckled. "Did you see the expression on her face when we took her out to the corral and she saw Tornado with that big red bow tied around her neck? She hugged me so tight she liked to choke me."

"She's a very exuberant child." Mariah crossed the room and plucked the stocking from the chair arm. "She is also messy."

Sherman took the stocking from her hand and tossed it into the chair. "Mariah, I have something for you." He put his hand in his pocket and drew out a small, velvet bag with a drawstring. "I didn't want to give this to you in front of everyone."

"Oh, Mr. Butler, I can't—" Mariah ran her palms down the sides of her coat.

"I want you to know that I love you more today than I did yesterday, and I reckon I'll probably love you more tomorrow than I do today." He turned the small bag around in his big hand. "Anyway, I'm not going to ask you to marry me again. I reckon once is enough for that."

Mariah clasped her hands together. "I don't know what to say."

"I know you don't. That's why I'm giving you until after the roundup to give me your answer." He took her hand in his. "I want you to take this. When you make up your mind, if the answer is yes, put it on your finger. That way, I'll know."

He placed the bag in her hand and closed her fingers around it. Leaning down he brushed her lips with a light but fervent kiss. Then he left the warmth of the house, but the warmth in his heart remained with him all the way home.

seventeen

In mid-February, a blizzard raced across the Kansas prairie dumping two feet of snow and forcing the cancellation of school. Mariah and Hope were housebound for two weeks. Mariah spent most of the time praying and reading her Bible.

One night, while Hope slept, she clutched the small, black velvet bag that contained the fulfillment of all her dreams as she read from the black, leather-bound book. She turned to the verse that had come to mean so much to her. *"For I know the thoughts I think toward you, saith the Lord, thoughts of peace, and not of evil, to give you an expected end."*

Mariah reflected over the past few weeks. She and Hope had spent the first day of 1894 at the Circle C. The Nolans were there, too. Mariah had accepted Mac's invitation to join them on the roundup. When Mac shared the news with everyone else, Carrie looked crestfallen.

After New Year's Day, Lucas and Carrie were always at the ranch for Sunday dinners. Occasionally Mariah would catch Carrie watching her with pain-filled eyes. At those times, Mariah's heart ached for the young woman. God in His infinite mercy and boundless love had given Mariah much more than she had ever dreamed possible. Hope would be enough. As much as she loved Sherman Butler, and she did love him, she would not come between Carrie and her father. Kneeling beside her chair, she thanked God for Hope. Then, with tears streaming down her face, she released the only man she had ever loved. She arose, and with a new determination, she sat at the small writing desk in her parlor and penned a short letter to the principal of her old school in Ohio.

ঌ

Two days later, after some of the snow had melted, Joanna came to visit. Sitting in Mariah's kitchen with teacups in hand and a full plate of sugar cookies between them, they caught up on the last two weeks.

"Not much happened." Joanna took a second cookie. "You make the best cookies in the state of Kansas. Anyway, as I was saying, not much happened, so I did a lot of thinking. You know what we need in Cedar Bend, Mariah? A library."

"A library?"

"Mmm-hmm. I think we should start a library." Joanna brushed cookie crumbs from her fingers. "So what do you think?"

"I think it's a wonderful idea." Mariah thought of the small library at school. "What books we have at school are excellent, but there are so few of them. Mark has already read everything."

"That's one reason I thought of a library. I've loaned Mark almost every book we own. The only ones left are Daddy's medical books." She took another cookie. "Mariah, would you please put those away before I eat the whole plateful? Anyway, learning to read has opened a whole new world for him. Can you believe he's halfway through the Old Testament?"

"Mark is a very bright young man," Mariah commented as she transferred cookies from the plate to a cookie jar. She put the lid on and got up to place the jar on the counter. Sitting back down across from Joanna, she smiled. "I hear he's sweet on you."

"Sweet? On me?" Joanna's rosy cheeks flushed a shade darker. "Whoever told you that?"

"A certain little pitcher with big ears."

"And an even bigger mouth!" Joanna exclaimed. "I told you when she started talking we would have to be careful what we said around her."

"It seems Mark's little sister told her that he is really sweet on you." Mariah grinned. "Mr. Butler says he has noticed a special gleam in Mark's eye when he looks at you."

"I guess Mr. Butler would recognize that gleam if anybody would," Joanna teased. "Daddy says he wishes you would marry the poor man and put him out of his misery."

Mariah's face flared bright red. She returned to their original subject before Joanna had a chance to say more. "About this library. Where would we put it?"

"I'm not sure." Joanna's expression was thoughtful. "We need a building, and that will take money. Then we'll need to buy books. I thought you might have some ideas. You are going to help me with this, aren't you?"

"I would like to, but I'm not sure I'll be able to be of much assistance." Mariah folded her hands on the table. "I may not be here after this school year ends."

"Oh, Mariah, why not? I thought you would marry Mr. Butler and stay in Cedar Bend forever."

"I would like to stay, but I'm not sure I'll be able to." She felt two tears slide down her cheeks.

Joanna's brown eyes brimmed. "Tell me about it."

Mariah told the younger woman everything, concluding with her struggles of the last week. "I love him with all my heart, Joanna, but I can't marry him. I can't build a life with Sherman on the ashes of Carrie's unhappiness. Yesterday I wrote to the principal of my old school and asked if they have an opening. If I receive a favorable reply from him I will take Hope and move back to Ohio."

"You can't go back, Mariah." Joanna dabbed at her tears with a napkin. "You have no friends in Ohio."

"But I will have," Mariah said with a confidence she didn't completely feel.

"But they won't love you like we do."

"My dear friend, before I came to Kansas I didn't know what love was."

"But you do now."

"Yes, I do." Mariah covered Joanna's hand with hers. "From you I have learned the love of a friend. With Gladys and her family I have experienced the love of family. With Hope I have come to understand one of the most precious loves of all, the love of a mother for her child. And, with Sherman, I have been allowed a glimpse of the love between a man and a woman. I wouldn't take anything for the time I have spent here, Joanna."

"You can't leave, Mariah," Joanna protested tearfully. "You have so many friends in Cedar Bend. Your students adore you. Mark thinks you are the most wonderful teacher on the face of the earth. You have no one in Ohio."

"Joanna, there is a verse in Jeremiah that says God has our future planned. I read that verse the morning I received the offer of the teaching position here. It didn't mean anything to me then, but now it does. I know God brought me here, and if it is His will I go back to Ohio, then I know He must have a reason." She squeezed Joanna's hand before releasing it. "Now, let's dry our tears and start planning your library."

A half hour later, when Hope wandered into the kitchen clutching Jake in one arm and looking for a snack, Mariah and Joanna were busy making lists. The little girl climbed up on Mariah's lap and shared her cookie with the doll.

Mariah and Joanna took their plans for a library to Gladys Jacobs a few days later. Under her able guidance, the project began to take shape as winter neared a close.

❧

One morning Mariah spotted a fat robin in her front yard. Spring had finally arrived. The days passed quickly as Mariah tried not to dwell on her impending move back to Ohio. Before she knew it, April arrived.

The school year ended with a graduation ceremony for Mark Hopkins, Jay Braun, and Fred Carson. Since the school was too small to accommodate the crowd that was expected to attend, closing exercises were held in the church.

With Mabel Carson at the piano, the students of Miss Mariah Casey stood at the front of the room and sang "Battle Hymn of the Republic." At the conclusion of the song, Dr. Tom Brady gave a short speech praising the accomplishments of the three young men. Then Sherman Butler, acting as school board president, handed out their diplomas. When he shook the hands of Jay and Fred and congratulated them, the applause was long and loud. Then Mark walked up, and the crowd rose to their feet to give the young man a thunderous ovation.

Sherman raised his hands, and the roar gradually died out as the crowd sat down.

"We are proud of what all three of these young men have accomplished," Sherman said. "They all received high marks in all subjects this year. The other young men have elected Mark Hopkins to speak in their behalf."

As the young man stood in front of the crowd, Mariah's heart swelled with pride. Six months ago when Mark walked into her classroom, he knew his alphabet but little else. He had completed eight grades in one school year, an almost unbelievable accomplishment.

"From the time I was a little shaver it was my dream to learn to read," he said. "After the crops were planted last spring, Pop took me aside and told me he wanted me to go to school. For many years I had prayed for this day. Now that the time had come, I knew it was impossible. Like Moses I could look into the Promised Land, but I couldn't enter. Do you know what stood in my way?" The young man laughed. "Pride, folks. It didn't overly bother me that I would be sitting at a table beside my six-year-old sister. But I could not abide the thought of someone I had known all my life—someone younger than myself—teaching me to read."

His gaze settled on Carrie. "I know you were a fine teacher,

Carrie. But I was mighty happy when Lucas took you out of the schoolroom." Laughter rippled through the crowd. "Carrie and I have been friends for years." Mark smiled. "I hope we always will be."

Carrie nodded an affirmation before Mark continued. "Jeremiah 29:11 says, 'For I know the thoughts that I think toward you, saith the Lord, thoughts of peace, and not of evil, to give you an expected end.' That verse is certainly true. Last September, God answered my prayers and sent me a miracle. When I saw Miss Casey at the dinner the town held to welcome her to Cedar Bend, I knew she would be the one to teach me to read. And I was right. I couldn't even tell you how many recesses and lunch breaks she gave up to teach me to read and write.

"Today I want to thank three very special people who made it possible for me to realize my dream. Mom and Pop, thank you for making the sacrifices and sending me to school.

"Miss Casey, on behalf of Fred and Jay, I want to thank you for the time you devoted to the three of us. You make learning an adventure. Would you please say a few words?"

Mariah rose and moved to stand beside Mark. The crowd erupted in applause. She waited patiently until the room grew still before attempting to speak. "For eighteen years I taught second graders. Facing a roomful of children of varying ages was an overwhelming experience. I didn't know how I would ever teach such a diversified group.

"I want you all to know that this last school year has been the most rewarding of my career. You have wonderful children. I have come to love every one of them. Teaching these young people has been a delight." Knowing this was the last time she would stand before the people she had come to love, Mariah ended abruptly. "I wish to thank you all for being here today to honor these three young men."

She returned to her seat. Pastor Carson offered the closing

prayer. The congregation sang "God Be with You." The program was over.

Mariah was immediately surrounded by her students and their parents. After the crowd thinned out, Joanna hugged her and whispered, "You are leaving?"

Mariah blinked back tears and nodded. "I got a letter from Principal Sterns yesterday."

"Have you told Mr. Butler?"

"No, not yet. I thought I would after the roundup."

Tears welled up in Joanna's brown eyes. "Don't go. Please, Mariah, don't go."

Neither one of the women knew Sherman was there until he spoke. "Don't go where?"

They both looked up at the tall rancher. "Nowhere," Mariah said. "We were talking about the roundup, and one thing and another."

"I see." He put his arm around Mariah's shoulders and gave her a brief hug. "I'm proud of you, Miss Casey."

"Thank you, Mr. Butler." Mariah managed a shaky smile. "Your approval means more to me than you will ever know."

Hope chose that moment to run up and fling her arms around Mariah's legs. "Mama, Miss Carrie says when she was a little girl like me she wore overnalls on the roundup. Can I have overnalls? Pul-eeze, Mama."

Mariah glanced at Carrie standing behind Hope, then smiled down into the little girl's upturned face. "I made you some divided skirts. Remember?"

"But I wants overnalls." Hope released Mariah and grasped Carrie's hand. "I wants to be a cowboy like Miss Carrie."

Mariah sighed. "If Harris's has overalls your size, I'll buy you a couple of pairs. All right?"

"Thank you, Mama." Hope flung her arms around Mariah. "I gots to tell L. K. and Julie I gets overnalls."

Mariah watched her daughter run off to join her friends.

"She's an adorable little girl," Carrie said. "You have done wonders with her, Miss Casey."

"Thank you, Mrs. Nolan."

"Since we are going to be spending the next week together, don't you think you should call me Carrie?"

"Yes, I would like that." Mariah hesitated for a heartbeat. "If you will call me Mariah."

"I have to go. Lucas is waiting for me." Carrie smiled. "I'll see you bright and early in the morning, Mariah."

"Yes. Good afternoon, Carrie."

Carrie actually smiled at her! Could Sherman's daughter actually be accepting her? Mariah turned to share this small victory with Sherman and found he and Joanna had both wandered away while she was talking to Carrie. Well, never mind. She couldn't allow her thoughts to stray in that direction anyway. She had already made up her mind to leave Cedar Bend. Right now she had to collect her daughter and go to the mercantile. Hope needed *overnalls*.

eighteen

The night before the spring roundup, Mariah and Hope slept in Carrie's old bedroom at the Circle C. It was still dark outside when Mariah rose and dressed. With Hope still sound asleep, she joined Mac in the kitchen. After a hastily prepared and eaten breakfast, she went back to the bedroom. Hope barely stirred when she scooped her and Jake up and carried them to the chuck wagon she and Mac had stocked the previous day.

As soon as Hope was settled on the bed inside the wagon, Sherman assisted Mariah onto the high seat beside Mac. "You look mighty fetchin' this morning, Miss Casey." His lips brushed against her ear.

Mariah blushed. She still felt uncomfortable in the divided skirt Joanna had insisted she make for the roundup. "Thank you, Mr. Butler."

Cyrus and the other men rode on ahead, while Sherman, Lucas, and Carrie rode beside the chuck wagon for a while. Then, tiring of the slow pace, they, too, rode on. Mariah hadn't slept well, and sitting beside Mac as they jostled and creaked across the prairie, she fought to keep her eyes open.

"Don't go, Mariah." Mac's sudden outburst jerked Mariah awake. The little man and Joanna were the only ones Mariah had told of her plans to leave Cedar Bend. "Sherm needs you."

"Mac, we've discussed this before." Mariah blinked back tears. "You know how I feel."

"Whut about how Sherm feels? He loves you, Mariah. Why, his face jist plum lights up when he looks at you. I ain't never seen him as happy as he has been these last few months."

"Please, Mac, there is no need to discuss this further. Didn't you tell me what can't be cured must be endured? That's what I'm trying to do, endure. Please help me to get through this."

Mac grumbled a bit under his breath, but the remainder of the trip passed in silence.

ঽ

The eastern sky was a symphony of pink and gold when Mariah and Hope set out with a bushel basket to collect cow chips.

Hope wrinkled her nose when Mariah bent to pick up the first dried chip in a gloved hand. "Pew-eee! You know what them things is, Mama?"

"They are fuel for our fire." Mariah added a second chip to the one in the basket.

"Uh-uh. Them is not fool. You know where them things come from?"

"Hope, where they came from is not important. People living on the prairie had to adapt. The brave pioneers who settled our land used what was at hand in order to survive. Why don't we pretend we're pioneers?"

"Uh-uh." Hope had insisted on having her hair braided like Carrie's. When she shook her head, the single, long braid switched back and forth. "I don't want to be no pie-neer. Does you want to be a pie-neer, Jake?" She consulted the doll clutched in the crook of her right arm. "Jake don't want to be no pie-neer neither. Me an' Jake wants to be cowboys like Miss Carrie."

"We'll see." Mariah picked up the basket, which was now full. "Let's go back to camp. Mac needs our help."

Hope trudged along at her side. "Mama, when Mistah Butlah is my daddy, he'll let me an' Jake be cowboys."

Mariah glanced down at the little girl. How was she going to tell Hope that Mr. Butler would never be her daddy? A month after the roundup they would be in Ohio. All the people they loved would be left behind in Cedar Bend. How could Hope—how could she—go on without Sherman and Mac and Joanna? And what of her family? What would she do without Gladys? And Carrie? Hope adored Carrie. *What can't be cured must be endured.* How, oh how, were they ever going to endure being separated from everyone they loved?

&

Every day Mac and Mariah loaded up and moved the chuck wagon to a new location. The roundup was noisy and dirty. The milling of hundreds of cows and horses kept an almost constant dust cloud rising over the camp. At night Mariah tumbled into the bed in the chuck wagon beside Hope, so tired she barely had strength to pull off her boots. At four o'clock in the morning, she forced herself from bed to begin all over.

The third morning they were out, Mariah stood behind a long table helping Mac serve breakfast. When she handed Carrie her plate, the young woman turned chalk white. Clapping a hand over her mouth, she stumbled away from the table, with Lucas close on her heels. That morning Carrie stayed in camp with Mac and Mariah. By the time the men brought in the first catch, she seemed to have recovered enough to go out and round up strays.

The same thing happened the following two mornings. After lunch, Carrie rode out with Lucas. Hope was taking the afternoon nap her mother insisted on, and Mac and Mariah were preparing for the final move of the roundup.

"I am concerned about Carrie," Mariah said. "She is so sick in the morning. I don't think she should be out in the afternoon in all that dust and heat."

"She probably ort not," Mac agreed. "But I wouldn't worry too much 'bout the little lady."

"She's so sick, Mac."

"I seen this sickness afore." Mac grinned. "Ain't nothin' time won't take keer of."

"You don't think what she has is contagious, do you?"

"I don't reckon so." The little man chuckled. "I'd reckon in 'bout seven months er so the little lady is gonna be a ma."

"You mean Carrie is—oh, my!" Mariah blushed bright crimson. "Carrie is with child? Oh, Mac! How wonderful! Do you think she knows?"

"I'd reckon not. If she did, she wouldn't be lookin' so woebegone."

"Maybe you should tell her." Mariah shook her head. "No, that wouldn't be proper. Somebody should tell her."

"I'd reckon she'll figure it out in due time."

❧

The next morning, Mariah saw that Carrie was sick, again. After helping serve the noontime meal, she moped around camp instead of going out with the men to round up the last of the strays. While Mariah and Mac washed the last of the tin pie plates, she sat on a low stool, watching them.

Mariah excused herself to put Hope down for a nap inside the chuck wagon. When she rejoined Mac and Carrie, they were deep in a conversation that ceased as soon as they saw her. Mariah expelled a deep breath as she sat down for some much-needed rest before beginning supper preparations. "I have never worked so hard in my life."

Mac smiled. "You've did a fine job, Mariah."

"Mariah, would you like to go down to the creek with me?" Carrie asked. "We could take a bath while the men are gone."

"My hair feels like it has ten pounds of dirt in it." Mariah ran a hand over the coronet of braids that encircled her head. "But I don't want to wake Hope. She is a regular little bear if she doesn't have her nap."

"I'll watch Hope," Mac offered. "You go on with the little lady."

Mariah put up only a token argument before going to collect a towel, a blanket, a bar of scented soap, and a change of clothes.

On the banks of the shallow creek, the two women stripped down to their sleeveless, knee-length, cotton-knit union suits and walked into the water. After they bathed and washed their hair, they waded to shore. Concealed by the blankets, they changed to fresh underwear, then dressed. After spreading the blankets in the sun, they sat down to dry their hair. Fortunately, Carrie had remembered to bring a hairbrush.

"I have been trying to get up the courage to talk to you." Carrie turned to face Mariah, the sun glinting red-gold off her damp hair. Tears sparkled in her dark eyes. "I have been so rude to you, Mariah. Can you ever forgive me?"

"Oh, Carrie! There is nothing to forgive. I'm the one who should be begging forgiveness. I was so hateful when I came to Cedar Bend. The first time I saw you I thought you were so beautiful. You reminded me of my—of someone I once knew." Tears welled up in Mariah's own eyes, and she hastily blinked them away. "I could make all manner of excuses, but I won't. My behavior was inexcusable."

"You are such a good teacher. Everyone was always bragging on you. I was so jealous." Carrie sniffled. "It all seems so unimportant now."

"I've been a teacher for many years, Carrie. After only one year, you couldn't expect to know everything it took me eighteen years to learn."

"I know." Carrie wiped the tears away with her fingertips. "I couldn't stand it when I saw that Papa was falling in love with you. I thought he was being unfaithful to Mama."

Mariah took a deep breath. "I would never do anything to come between you and your father, Carrie. Surely you know that."

"You love my papa, don't you?"

"Yes, I do. Very much."

Two drops of liquid crystal rolled down Carrie's cheeks. "Mac told me you were going back to Ohio. Is that true?"

Mariah glanced down before raising her head and looking directly into Carrie's tear-filled eyes. "Hope and I will be leaving shortly after the roundup ends."

"Don't go, Mariah." Carrie threw both arms around the older woman. "Please stay. Papa loves you so much." She burrowed her head into Mariah's shoulder.

Mariah put her arms around Carrie and held the young woman close while she sobbed. "I have never been sick in my life. Never." The words came amid heartrending sobs. "I'm so sick. I know I'm going to die. I don't want to leave Lucas and Papa and everybody else, Mariah. But I know I'm going to have to. After I'm gone Papa is going to need you."

Mariah held Carrie and patted her back until the sobs became occasional hiccupy shudders, then died away. The young woman pulled away and wiped at her eyes with the backs of her hands. "I'm trying to not be afraid, but I can't help but be. Mama died young. I remember how sick she was. I think I may have the same illness."

"Carrie, listen to me! You aren't going to die." She took the young woman's hand in hers. "If what Mac suspects is true, your illness isn't about death. It's about life."

"Life?"

"Life." Mariah smiled and squeezed the younger woman's hand. "A new life. Mac believes you display all the symptoms of being with child."

"With child?" A glorious smile lit Carrie's face. "I'm going to have a baby! Lucas and I are going to have a baby! Of course. I remember how sick Lucille was. And Gretchen says she thought she was going to die for a month or so. Oh, Mariah!"

"Carrie, I won't be here when the baby's born, but will you write and let me know about him?"

"Won't be here?" Carrie turned a wide-eyed gaze on the older woman. "What do you mean you won't be here? Aren't you going to marry Papa?"

Mariah picked at her skirt. "I told you I wouldn't come between you and your father. Now that you know you aren't dying—well, I thought—"

"The selfish little brat that said all those terrible things to you deserves to lose you, Mariah. But not my baby. He needs a grandmother. And not Papa. Papa needs a wife. I need you, too, Mariah. Please say you will stay and be my baby's grandma and Papa's wife and my friend. I want you with me when my baby is born, Mariah. Please say yes. Please say you will stay here with us."

"For I know the plans I have for you, saith the Lord." Drops of saltwater fell on Mariah's hands. Tears of joy. "Yes," she said, looking into Carrie's dark eyes. "Yes, Carrie, I will stay."

❧

That evening after supper the cowhands gathered around to sing and swap tall tales. Mariah left Carrie to watch Hope. Then she asked Sherman to go for a walk with her. As they wandered along the banks of the creek, he took her hand in his.

"Have you made a decision, Mariah?"

"Yes, I have." Inside the pocket of her skirt Mariah ran her thumb around the band of gold that encircled her finger.

They stopped walking. Sherman put his fingers under her chin, lifting her face until their eyes met. "Will you be my wife, Mariah?"

Mariah withdrew her left hand from her pocket and held it up. A moonbeam glanced off the diamond on her finger.

"Ya-hoo!" Sherman hugged her so tight she thought her ribs might crack. A shower of kisses rained down on her face before his lips met hers. She clung to him and returned his kisses with all the love in her heart.

When they walked into camp hand in hand, Mac smiled. "Wal, have you got somethin' you want to tell us?" the little man asked.

"I have an announcement to make." Sherman grinned and put his arm around the woman at his side. "Miss Mariah Casey has finally agreed to be my wife. The wedding will be Sunday afternoon, May 14, at the Community Church. You are all invited."

The men gathered round laughing and congratulating Sherman. Carrie hugged her father, then put her arms around Mariah. Hope tugged on Sherman's pant leg. He lifted the little girl into his arms.

"Are you gonna be my daddy?" she asked.

"I sure am."

"Good." Hope planted a wet kiss on his cheek. "Can I be a cowboy?" She batted her big blue eyes. "Pul-eeze, Daddy?"

epilogue

"White satin?" Mariah laughed. It seemed she laughed a lot these days. "Don't you think I'm a bit old for white satin?"

"There is no reason you shouldn't wear white, Mariah." Carrie shook her head firmly as if to emphasize the words.

"I think you will be beautiful in white." Joanna wrote on the pad of paper as if the matter was settled. "White satin. All right." She looked around Mariah's kitchen table at the other three women gathered to help plan Mariah and Sherman's wedding. "What else shall we put on our list?"

"A veil," Lucille said. "You need a veil, Cousin Mariah."

"Really, girls! Veils are for young brides. If I agree to the white satin, will you agree to a simple hat?"

The three young women looked at her; then Carrie said, "I have a wonderful idea. You can wear my veil. I wore Mama's wedding dress, but my veil was my something new. It can be your something borrowed."

"Perfect," Joanna exclaimed. She made a note on the pad of paper. "Now, what about flowers for the bridal bouquet?"

Mariah sat down with a soft plop in the chair behind her. She let her gaze linger on each girl before her and smiled as they continued to chatter, making plans for her wedding without her input. Hope wandered into the kitchen and stopped beside Mariah's chair. As she leaned against her, Mariah slipped an arm around her and drew her close. *"For I know the thoughts that I think toward you, saith the Lord, thoughts of peace, and not of evil, to give you an expected end."*

❧

Mariah walked down the aisle with slow, measured steps

behind Hope. Her daughter dropped rose petals with precision, keeping her head bent to the task. Mariah lifted her gaze to the front where Sherman stood waiting, tall and handsome. Her breath caught in her throat as her old insecurities tried to gain a hold. Then she saw the love-light in his eyes as he met and held her gaze with his and knew that for whatever reason, Sherman Butler loved her as much as she loved him.

When he took her hand in his, Hope stepped to the front pew and sat down. Mariah smiled at her beaming face, then turned with her hand sheltered in Sherman's to take the vows that would forever bind them together.

❧

"You may kiss the bride." Sherman enclosed Mariah in his arms and claimed her lips under his. When he lifted his head, his smile was wide as his arm kept her close to his side.

"May I introduce to you, Mr. and Mrs. Sherman Butler." The minister's joyous words brought smiles and laughter as the congregation stood and Hope joined her parents.

With Hope leading the way, Mariah walked beside her husband past their friends and family while Carrie and Lucas followed. In less than a year she had gone from a friendless, bitter woman to a bride with more friends than she could count.

The dearest man on earth loved her. She had two beautiful daughters and a wonderful son-in-law. In a few months she would become a grandmother. *"For I know the thoughts that I think toward you, saith the Lord, thoughts of peace, and not of evil, to give you an expected end."* What a wonderful God she served! Mariah's soft laughter brought a smile from her new husband.

A Letter To Our Readers

Dear Reader:

In order that we might better contribute to your reading enjoyment, we would appreciate your taking a few minutes to respond to the following questions. We welcome your comments and read each form and letter we receive. When completed, please return to the following:

Fiction Editor
Heartsong Presents
PO Box 719
Uhrichsville, Ohio 44683

1. Did you enjoy reading *Mariah's Hope* by M. J. Conner?
   ❑ Very much! I would like to see more books by this author!
   ❑ Moderately. I would have enjoyed it more if

   _____

   _____

   _____

2. Are you a member of **Heartsong Presents**? ❑ Yes ❑ No
   If no, where did you purchase this book? _____

   _____

3. How would you rate, on a scale from 1 (poor) to 5 (superior), the cover design? _____

4. On a scale from 1 (poor) to 10 (superior), please rate the following elements.

   ____ Heroine   ____ Plot
   ____ Hero   ____ Inspirational theme
   ____ Setting   ____ Secondary characters

5. These characters were special because? _____

_____

_____

6. How has this book inspired your life? _____

_____

_____

7. What settings would you like to see covered in future
   Heartsong Presents books? _____

_____

_____

8. What are some inspirational themes you would like to see
   treated in future books? _____

_____

_____

9. Would you be interested in reading other **Heartsong
   Presents** titles? ❏ Yes ❏ No

10. Please check your age range:
    ❏ Under 18   ❏ 18-24
    ❏ 25-34   ❏ 35-45
    ❏ 46-55   ❏ Over 55

Name _____

Occupation _____

Address _____

City, State, Zip_____

Heart♥ng

HEARTSONG PRESENTS TITLES AVAILABLE NOW:

Presents

HEARTSONG
PRESENTS

If you love Christian romance…

$10.⁹⁹

You'll love Heartsong Presents' inspiring and faith-filled romances by today's very best Christian authors…DiAnn Mills, Wanda E. Brunstetter, and Yvonne Lehman, to mention a few!

When you join Heartsong Presents, you'll enjoy four brand-new, mass market, 176-page books—two contemporary and two historical—that will build you up in your faith when you discover God's role in every relationship you read about!

Imagine…four new romances every four weeks—with men and women like you who long to meet the one God has chosen as the love of their lives…all for the low price of $10.99 postpaid.

Mass Market 176 Pages

To join, simply visit www.heartsong presents.com or complete the coupon below and mail it to the address provided.

✄- -

YES! Sign me up for Heartsong!

NEW MEMBERSHIPS WILL BE SHIPPED IMMEDIATELY!
Send no money now. We'll bill you only $10.99 postpaid with your first shipment of four books. Or for faster action, call 1-740-922-7280.

NAME_____

ADDRESS_____

CITY_____ STATE _____ ZIP _____

MAIL TO: HEARTSONG PRESENTS, P.O. Box 721, Uhrichsville, Ohio 44683
or sign up at WWW.HEARTSONGPRESENTS.COM